Jane shook out her wet skirts. The thin muslin clung to her body, which was as slender and delicate as ever, and just as alluring to him. But what caught his avid attention was the look on her face. She appeared so alive, so happy and free as she laughed. Her eyes sparkled.

He remembered how it had felt that first time he took her hand, as if her warmth and innocence could be his. As if the life he had always led, the only life he knew, wasn't the only way he had to be. That he could find another path—with her.

Maybe it was this place, this strange, ramshackle, warm-hearted place, that had given his wife that air of laughing, welcoming life. Because here she bloomed. With him she had faded, and he had faded with her. Yet here she was his Jane again.

His hope. And he had never, ever wanted to hope again.

BANCROFTS OF BARTON PARK

Two sisters, two scandals, two sizzling love affairs

Country girls at heart, Jane and Emma Bancroft
are a far cry from the perfectly coiffed, glossy debutantes
that grace most of Society.

But soon they come to realise that,
country girl and debutante alike, no lady is
immune to the charms of a dashing rogue!

**Don't miss this enthralling new duet
from Amanda McCabe**

starting with Jane's story

THE RUNAWAY COUNTESS

Look for Emma's story

coming in December 2013

RUNNING FROM SCANDAL

THE RUNAWAY COUNTESS

Amanda McCabe

MILLS & BOON®

First published in Great Britain 2013
by Mills & Boon, an imprint of Harlequin (UK) Limited.
Harlequin (UK) Limited, Eton House, 18-24 Paradise Road,
Richmond, Surrey TW9 1SR

© Ammanda McCabe 2013

ISBN: 978 0 263 89848 4

Harlequin (UK) policy is to use papers that are natural, renewable and recyclable products and made from wood grown in sustainable forests. The logging and manufacturing process conform to the legal environmental regulations of the country of origin.

Printed and bound in Spain
by Blackprint CPI, Barcelona

Amanda McCabe wrote her first romance at the age of sixteen—a vast epic, starring all her friends as the characters, written secretly during algebra class. She's never since used algebra, but her books have been nominated for many awards, including the RITA®, *RT Book Reviews* Reviewers' Choice Award, the Booksellers Best, the National Readers' Choice Award, and the Holt Medallion. She lives in Oklahoma, with a menagerie of two cats, a pug and a bossy miniature poodle, and loves dance classes, collecting cheesy travel souvenirs, and watching the Food Network—even though she doesn't cook.

Visit her at http://ammandamccabe.tripod.com and www.riskyregencies.blogspot.com

Did you know that some of these novels are also available as eBooks? Visit www.millsandboon.co.uk

AUTHOR NOTE

I was so excited to find out this year is the 200th anniversary of the publication of *Pride and Prejudice*! It was discovering the world of Jane Austen that introduced me to the wonders of the Regency period. I found a battered paperback copy of *Emma* tucked away on a shelf in my grandmother's house when I was about ten and, after reading it, immediately ran to the library to see what else this mysterious Jane Austen had written. The librarian gave me all the other novels, as well as two Austen biographies and a book called *Life in Regency England*. I was hooked.

I've always loved the settings and themes of Austen's timeless stories—family, community, characters struggling to find ways to stay true to themselves and still meet the expectations of the society around them. And heroines determined to marry for love and find happiness in the face of overwhelming pressure to find stability at all costs. It's been so much fun to explore the same ideas with the Bancroft sisters, Jane and Emma, and their handsome heroes! That's the best part of writing historical romance—exploring a world so different from my own, but also so very similar in our emotions and dreams (just with better clothes!).

And I have Jane Austen—and the wonderful librarian who recognised a new Austen mania and helped me make it grow—to thank for all those hours of delight and joy. Happy anniversary, Lizzie and Darcy!

DEDICATION

To librarians everywhere,
for working so hard to open the world to us…

Prologue

London—1810
The most spectacular marriage in London...

Jane Fitzwalter, the Countess of Ramsay, almost laughed aloud as she read those words. They looked so solid in their black, smudged newsprint, right there in the gossipy pages of the *Gazette* for everyone to see. If it was written there, so many people thought, it had to be true.

Once she had even believed in it herself, for a brief moment. But not now. Now the words were hollow and false, mocking her and all her silly dreams.

The beautiful Ramsays, so young, so

wealthy, so fashionable. They had a grand London house where they held grand balls, great crushes with invitations fervently sought by every member of the *ton*. A grand country house where they held grand shooting parties, and the laughter and merriment went on until dawn. Lady Ramsay's hats and gowns, stored in their own grand wardrobe room, were emulated by all the ladies who aspired to fashion in London.

And everyone knew the tale of their marriage. How the young Lord Ramsay glimpsed the even younger Miss Jane Bancroft across the crowded salon full of tall, waving plumes at her Court presentation and strode past the whole gawking gathering to demand an introduction. How they danced together at two private balls and once at Almack's and went driving once in Hyde Park, and Lord Ramsay insisted she marry him. Her guardian wasn't sure, having doubts about the couple's youth and short acquaintance, but they threatened to elope and the next thing society knew they were attending a grand, glittering wedding at St George's.

Grand, grand, grand. The life of the beautiful Ramsays was the envy of everyone.

But Lady Ramsay, now slightly less young and much less naïve, would gladly sell all that grandness for a farthing. She would give it all away to go back to that sunny day in Hyde Park, her shoulder pressed close to Hayden's as they sat together in his curricle and laughed. As they held hands secretly under the cover of her parasol. On that day the world seemed to stretch before her in glorious, golden promise. That day seemed to promise everything she had dreamed of— love, security, a place to belong, someone who needed her.

If only they could start again there and move forwards in a whole different way. But sadly that was impossible. Life would simply go on again as it had done already, because they were the Ramsays and that was the way of their world.

But she was heartily sick of this world of theirs. She had expected that Hayden's title would give them security in the world, a security she never had with her own family, but she had been foolish. She hadn't realised how a title took over everything else, became everything. That a title gathered empty friends, empty marriages.

Jane let the paper fall to the floor beside her bed and slid back down amid the heaps of pillows. It was surely very late at night by now. Her maid had tried to close the satin curtains at the windows, but Jane wouldn't let her. She liked seeing the darkness outside, it felt safe and comforting, like a thick blanket wrapped around her. The moon, a silvery sliver sliding towards the horizon, blinked at her.

Out there beyond her quiet chamber there were balls still twirling on with music and dancing and wine, laughter and conversation. Once she would have been in the very midst of one of those balls, laughing and dancing with the rest or gaily losing in the card room. Now the thought of it made her feel faintly ill.

She rolled on to her side to face the crackling blaze in the marble fireplace and her gaze fell on the bottle of laudanum the doctor had left for her. It would take away all the memories, draw her off to a dream-land, but she didn't want that, either. She had to think now, to face the truth no matter how painful it was.

She pressed her hand to her stomach, perfectly flat again beneath her linen nightdress. The tiny bump that had been growing there, filling her with such joy, was gone. It had been gone for days now, vanished as if it had never been. Lost in a flurry of agonising spasms—and Hayden was not with her. Again. When she lost their child, the third child she had lost so early, he was off gambling somewhere. And drinking, of course. Always drinking. Now there was only that hollow ache to remind her. She had failed in her duty. Again.

She couldn't go on like this any longer. She was cracking under the pressure of their grand lie. She had thought she was getting a new family with Hayden, yet she felt lonelier than she ever had before.

Suddenly she heard a sound from downstairs, a crash and a muffled voice. It was explosively loud in the silent house, for she had sent the servants to bed hours ago. Hayden wasn't expected back until dawn.

But it seemed he had come home early. Jane carefully climbed out of her bed and reached for a shawl to wrap around her shoulders. She slowly made her way out to the staircase landing and peered down to the hall below.

Hayden sat sprawled on the lower steps, the light of the lamp the butler had left on the pier table flickering over him. He had knocked over the umbrella stand, and parasols and walking sticks lay scattered over the black-and-white tiles of the floor.

Hayden studied them with a strangely sad look on his handsome face. The pattern of shadows and light carved his starkly elegant features into something mysterious, and for a moment he almost looked like the man she had married with such hope. Could it be possible he was as weary of this frantic life as she was? That they could somehow start again? Despite her cold disillusionment, she still dared to hope. Still dared to be irrational.

Jane took a step down the stairs and at the creak of the wooden tread Hayden looked up at her. For an instant she saw the stark look on his face, but then he grinned and the brief moment of reflection and hope was gone.

He pushed back a lock of his tousled black hair and held out his hand to her. The signet ring on his finger gleamed and she saw the brandy stain on his sleeve. 'Jane! My beautiful wife waits to greet me—how amazing.'

As Jane moved slowly down the stairs, she could smell the sweet-acrid scent of the brandy hovering around him like a cloud. 'I couldn't sleep,' she said. She hadn't been able to sleep for days and days.

'You should have come with me to the Westin rout, then,' he said. 'It was quite the crush.'

Jane gently smoothed back his hair and cupped her palm over his cheek. The faint roughness of his evening whiskers tickled her skin and the sky-blue of his eyes glowed in the shadows.

How very handsome he was, her husband. How her heart ached just to look at him. Once he had been everything she had ever wanted.

'So I see,' she said.

'Everyone asked about you there,' he answered. He turned his head to press a quick, careless kiss into her palm. 'You're missed by our friends.'

'Friends?' she murmured doubtfully. She barely knew the Westins, or anyone who had been there tonight. And they did not know her, not really. She always felt shy and uncomfortable at balls, another way she failed at being a countess. 'I don't feel like parties yet.'

'Well, I hope you will very soon. The Season is still young and we have a brace of invitations to respond to.' He kissed her hand again, but Jane had the distinct sense he didn't even feel her, see her. 'I hate it when you're ill, darling.'

Feeling a tiny spark of hope, Jane caught his hands in hers and said, 'Maybe we need a little holiday, a few weeks in the country with just us. I'm sure I would feel better in the fresh air. We could take my sister, Emma, from school to come see us. It's been so long since I was with Emma.'

As she thought about it she grew more excited. Yes, she was sure a holiday would be a wonderful thing. A time in the country at

Barton Park, just the three of them, no parties, no brandy. She and Hayden could talk again, as they used to, and be together—maybe make a new baby. Try one more time, despite her fears. They could leave the grand Ramsays behind and just be Hayden and Jane. That was what she had once hoped for so much.

But Hayden laughed at her words, as if she had just made some great joke. He let go of her hands and sprawled back on to the steps. 'Go off to the country now? Jane darling, it's the very midst of the Season. We can't possibly leave now.'

'But it could be—'

Hayden shook his head. 'Staying in London would do you more good than burying yourself in the country. You should go to parties with me again, enjoy yourself. Everyone expects it of you, of us.'

'Go to parties as you do?' Jane said bitterly as her faint, desperate hope faded away. Nothing had changed. Nothing *would* change.

'Yes, as I do. As my parents always did,'

he said. 'It's better than wallowing in misery alone at home.'

Jane wrapped her arms around herself, feeling suddenly hollow and empty. Cold. 'I am tired. Perhaps I will go away by myself to visit my sister. Poor Emma writes that she doesn't like her school and I miss her. I just need some time away from London. I want to go home to Barton Park for a while.'

Hayden closed his eyes as if he was weary of her and this conversation. Weary of her emotions. 'If you like, of course. You will have to return before our end-of-Season ball, though. Everyone expects that.'

Jane nodded, but she already knew she would not be back for any ball. She couldn't return to this life at all. She needed to find her own soul again, even if she couldn't make Hayden see that he needed to save his.

He gave a faint snore and Jane looked down to find that he had drifted to sleep right there on the stairs, in the middle of their conversation. His face looked so beautiful and peaceful, a faint smile on his lips as if he had already floated out of her life and into the one he had chosen for himself long before he met her. She leaned down and softly kissed his cheek and smoothed back his hair one last time.

'I'm sorry, Hayden,' she whispered. 'Forgive me.'

She rose to her feet and stepped over him, going back to her chamber and closing the door quietly behind her. It didn't even make a sound in the vast house that had never really been hers.

Hayden stared up at the ceiling far above his head, not seeing the elaborate, cake-icing whorls of white plaster. He barely felt the hard press of the stairs at his back, either, or the familiar feeling of a headache growing behind his eyes. All he could see, all he could think about, was Jane.

He closed his eyes and listened carefully, but she was long gone. There was only silence since she had tiptoed away and softly closed her chamber door behind her. Even his butler, Makepeace, had given up on him and left him lying there on the stairs. Cold air swept around him from the marble floor of the hall.

He had truly become what he never wanted to be—his parents.

Not that he was really like his father, oh, no. The elder earl had been all about responsibility and proper family appearances. It was Hayden's mother who had liked the parties, liked the forgetfulness of being in a noisy crowd. But they had both liked brandy and port too much and it killed his father in the end.

His mother, rest her giddy soul, was done in by childbirth, trying one last time to give his father another son.

A spasm of raw, burning pain flashed through Hayden as he remembered Jane's face, as white as the sheets she lay on after the first baby was gone, thin and drawn with pain.

'We can try again, Hayden,' she had said, reaching for his hand. 'The doctor says I am truly healthy, there's no reason it won't work next time. Please, Hayden, please stay with me.'

And he'd taken her trembling hand, murmured all the right, reassuring things, but inside he was shouting—*not again.* Never again. He couldn't hurt her again, couldn't see her go through what his mother had.

When he first saw Jane, saw the young, hopeful light in her pretty hazel eyes and the sweet pink blush in her cheeks, he felt something he had thought long dead stir inside of him. A curiosity, maybe, an excitement about life and what might happen next. It was more intoxicating than any wine, that feeling Jane gave him. And when he touched her hand, when she smiled up at him...

He only wanted that feeling she gave him to last for ever. He had to have her and he never stopped to think of the consequences. Until he was forced to.

He'd done Jane a great wrong in marrying her so quickly after they met, before she could see the real him. No matter what he did now it seemed he could not make her happy. He couldn't even see what she wanted, needed. She always looked at him so expectantly, so sadly, with those eyes of hers, as if she was waiting for something from him. Something he couldn't even begin to fathom.

So he ran back to what he *did* know, his friends and their never-ending parties. And

Jane grew sadder, especially when the babies were lost. Three of them now.

Hayden pushed himself slowly to his feet and made his careful way up the stairs. There was no sound beyond Jane's door, just that perfect, echoing silence. He pushed the door open and peered inside.

Jane lay on her side in the middle of the satin-draped bed countesses had slept in for decades. Her palm was tucked under her cheek, her thick, dark braid snaking over her shoulder. The moonlight fell over her face and he saw she was frowning even in her sleep. She looked so small, so vulnerable and alone.

Hayden knew he had let her down very badly. But he vowed he would never do it again, no matter what he had to do. Even if it meant letting her go.

'I promise you, Jane,' he whispered as she stirred in her sleep. 'I will never hurt you again.'

Chapter One

Three Years Later

Was it an earthquake in London?

That was surely the only explanation for the blasted pounding noise, because Hayden knew that no one in his household would dare to disturb him with such a sound in the middle of the night.

He rolled over on to his back in the tangled bedclothes and opened his eyes to stare up at the dark green canopy above his head. Pinpricks of light were trickling around the edges of the tightly closed window curtains, but surely it *was* still the middle of the night. He remembered coming home from the club with Harry and Edwards, stumbling through the streets singing, and somehow he had made it up the stairs and into bed. Alone.

Now he felt the familiar ache behind his eyes, made worse by that incessant banging noise.

The room itself wasn't shaking. He could see that now that he forced himself to be still. So it wasn't an earthquake. Someone was knocking at the bedroom door.

'Damn it all!' he shouted as he pushed himself off the bed. 'It is the middle of the night.'

'If you will beg pardon, my lord, you will find it is actually very near noon,' Makepeace said, calmly but firmly, from the other side of the door.

'The hell it is,' Hayden muttered. He found his breeches tangled up amid the twisted bedclothes and impatiently jerked them on. His shirt was nowhere to be found.

He glanced at the clock on the fireplace mantel, and saw that Makepeace was quite right. It was going on noon. He raked his hands through his tangled hair and jerked open the door.

'Someone had better be dead,' he said.

Makepeace merely blinked, his round, jowly face solemn as usual. He had been with Hayden's family for many years, having been promoted to butler even before Hayden's parents died when he was twelve. Makepeace had seen too much in the Fitzwalter household to ever be surprised.

'To my knowledge, my lord, no one has shuffled off this mortal coil yet,' Makepeace said. 'This letter just arrived.'

He held out his silver tray, which held one small, neatly folded missive. Hayden stared at it in disbelief.

'A letter?' he said. 'You woke me for *that*? Leave it with the rest of the post on the breakfast table and I'll read it later.'

He started to slam the door to go back to bed, but Makepeace adroitly slid his foot in. He proffered the tray again. 'You will want to read this right away, my lord. It's from Barton Park.'

Hayden wasn't sure he had heard Makepeace right. Perhaps he was still in bed, having a bizarre brandy-induced dream where letters arrived from Barton Park. 'What did you say?'

'If you will look at the return address, my lord, you will see it's from Barton Park,' Makepeace said. 'I thought you might want to see it right away.'

Hayden couldn't say anything. He merely nodded and took the letter carefully from the tray. He closed the door and stared down at the small, neatly folded missive. It glowed a snowy white in the dim, gloomy room, like some exotic and deadly snake about to strike.

It did indeed read 'JF, Barton Park' in a neat, looping handwriting he remembered all too well. The last time he received a letter from that address had been three years ago, when Jane wrote a brief note to tell him she had arrived at Barton Park and would be staying there until further notice. Since then he had sent her monthly bank drafts that were never cashed and he hadn't heard from her at all. He would only know she was alive because his agents reported it to him on a periodic basis.

Why would his estranged wife be writing to him today? And why did he feel a blasted, terrible spark of hope as he looked at the paper? Hope wasn't something he deserved. Not when it came to Jane.

The haze of last night's drink cleared in an instant as he stared down at the letter in his hand. All his senses seemed to sharpen, three years vanished and all he could see was Jane. The way the light glowed on her dark hair as she laughed with him in their sunlit bed. The rose-pink blush that washed over her cheeks when he teased her. The way she stared up at him, her eyes shining with emotion, as he made love to her.

The way all that heat and light had completely vanished, turned to cold, clear, hard ice, when she turned away from him. When she threw away their marriage and left him.

Now she was writing to him again.

Hayden slowly walked to the fireplace and propped the unopened letter on the mantel, next to the clock. Leaving it there, like a white, reproachful beacon, he went to the window to pull back the curtains and let the light in. When Jane left, it had been a chilly, rainy spring, the busiest part of the Season. Now summers and winters had passed, and it was almost summer again. A time of warmth and light, and long, lazy days.

What had Jane been doing all that time? He had tried not to think about that over those long three years, about Jane and what her life was like now. Every time she came through his mind he shoved her away, buried her in cards and drink, in late nights where if he didn't sleep he couldn't dream. They were better off apart. They had been so young and foolish when they married and she was safer away from him. He had convinced himself she was just a pale phantom.

Almost.

Hayden unlatched the window and pushed it open. Fresh air rushed into the stale room for the first time in days, a warm breeze that was another reminder that summer was coming. That his life really couldn't keep going on as it had, in a blurred succession of parties and drinking. That was the way it had always been, the way his parents' life had been. It was all he knew, all he had been taught. But what could take their place? Once he had known, or thought he had known, something different. But it was an illusion in the end.

Hayden turned away from the bright day outside and caught a glimpse of himself in the mirror across the room. For a second he didn't recognise himself. His black hair needed cutting and was tangled over his brow. He had lost weight and his breeches hung from his lean hips. His eyes were shadowed.

'Jane would never know you now, you disreputable bastard,' he told himself with a bitter laugh. He pulled open his wardrobe and reached for the first shirt hanging there. He pulled it over his head and splashed some cold water over his face. He wanted a brandy to fortify himself for reading Jane's letter, but there was none nearby.

He had to read it now.

Hayden took the letter from the mantel and broke the seal.

'Hayden,' it began. No 'dear' or 'beloved'. Right to the point.

It has been some time since I wrote and I am sorry for being rather quiet. Matters have been so very busy here. As you may remember, Barton Park has been neglected for some time and it has taken up so much of my attention. I believe I have made it quite comfortable again and Emma has left school to come stay with me permanently. We go along very well together and I hope that you are well too.

The reason I am writing is this. It has been a long while since we lived together as husband and wife. It occurred to me that we cannot go on this way for much longer. You are an earl and must have an heir, I know that very well. I am also well aware of how difficult and expensive a divorce would be. But you are a man of influence in London with many friends. If you wish to begin proceedings, I will not stop you in any way. My life here is a quiet one and scandal cannot touch it.

I will not stand in the way of your future. I trust that, in honour of what we once had, you will not stand in the way of mine.

Sincerely,

Jane.

Hayden was stunned. A divorce? Jane wrote him after all this time to say he should seek a divorce? He crumpled the letter in his fist and tossed it into the empty grate. A raw, burning fury swept through him, an anger he didn't understand. What had he expected would happen with Jane? Had he just thought they would go along in their strange twilight world for ever, married but not married?

The truth was he had avoided thinking about it at all. Now he saw he must. Jane was quite right. Even though he avoided considering his responsibilities as much as possible, he needed an heir. When Jane lost the babies, that hope was gone as well as their marriage. It was like his poor mother all over again, only Jane had luckily been spared the fate of dying trying to give her husband a spare to go with his heir. Jane was saved— because she wisely left. Yes, she was right about it all.

But something else was there, something she did not say in that polite, carefully worded little letter. He wasn't sure what it was, what was really going on with her, but he was sure there was more to this sudden plea for a divorce.

My life here is a quiet one and scandal cannot affect it.

How quiet *was* her life at Barton Park? He had heard nothing of how she really lived in the years since they had parted. No one ever saw her and, after the initial ripple of gossip over their separation, no one spoke of her. They treated him as if he was a single man again, as if Jane had never been. Now he wondered what she did. Why she wanted to be away from him in such a permanent way.

Suddenly he knew he had to see her again. He had to know what was really going on. She had left him, left their life together without a backward glance. He wouldn't let things be easy for her any longer.

No matter what Jane thought, she *was* still his wife. It was time she remembered that. Time they both remembered that.

Hayden strode to the door and pulled it open. 'Makepeace!' he shouted.

'My lord?' came the faint reply up the stairs. Makepeace always disapproved of

Hayden's strange habit of shouting out of doors.

'Call for my horse to be saddled. I am leaving for the country today.'

Chapter Two

'*Who is that?*'

Hayden's best friend, Lord John East-wood, looked around at Hayden's sudden question. It had been a long, dull day, hanging about at the royal Drawing Room, watching all that Season's crop of fresh young misses make their curtsies to the queen. John's sister, Susan, was one those misses and he had been recruited to help her. Hayden in return was recruited to help John survive the deadly dullness of it all.

Only for John would Hayden brave such a place and only after a stiff gulp of port. They had been friends ever since they were awkward schoolboys, drawn together by a *shared humour and love of parties. John's family took Hayden in on holidays when his own family was too busy for him.*

But even for the Eastwoods he was regretting venturing in there, to the over-gilded overheated room stuffed with girls in awkwardly hooped satin-and-lace gowns and towering plumes—and their sharp-eyed, avidly husband-hunting mamas.

A new young earl like Hayden was just a sitting duck, or a fox flushed out of hiding. He wanted to run.

Until he saw her.

She stood amid the gaggle of white-clad girls, overdressed just like them, with the tall headdress of white feathers in her dark hair threatening to overwhelm her slender figure. She was silent, carefully watching everything around her, but she drew his attention like the sudden flicker of a candle in the darkness.

She wasn't beautiful, not like so many of the pretty blonde shepherdess types clustered around her. She was too slim, too pale, with brown hair and a pointed chin, like a forest fairy. Yet she wore her ridiculous gown with an air of quiet, stylish dignity and her pink lips were curved in a little smile as if she had a secret joke no one else in the crowd could know.

And Hayden really, really wanted her to tell him what it was. What made her smile like that. No one had caught his attention so suddenly, so completely, in—well, ever. He had to find out who she was.

'Who is that?' Hayden asked again, and it seemed something in the urgency of his tone caught John's attention. John stopped grinning at his current flirtation, a certain Lady Eleanor Saunders, and turned to Hayden.

'Who is who?' John asked.

'That girl over there, in the white with the silver lace,' Hayden said impatiently.

'There are approximately fifty girls in white over there.'

'It's that one, of course.' Hayden turned to gesture to her, only to find that now she watched him. Her smile was gone and she looked a bit startled.

Her eyes were the strangest colour of golden-green, and they seemed to draw him in to her, closer and closer.

'The little brunette who is looking this way,' he said quietly, as if he feared to scare her away if he spoke too loudly. She had such a quiet, watchful delicacy to her.

'Oh, her. She is Miss Jane Bancroft, the niece of Lady Kenton.'

'You know her?' How could John know her and he could not?

'She had tea with Susan last week. It seems they met in the park and rather liked each other.' John gave Hayden a sharp glance of sudden interest. 'Why? Would you like to meet her?'

'Yes,' Hayden said simply. He couldn't stop looking at her, couldn't stop trying to decipher what was so immediately and deeply alluring about her.

'She's not your usual sort, is she?' John said.

'My usual sort?'

'You know. Dashing, colourful. Like Lady Marlbury. You've never looked twice at a deb before.'

Hayden couldn't even remember who Lady Marlbury was at the moment, even though she had been his sometimes-mistress for a *few weeks. Not when Miss Bancroft smiled at him, then looked shyly away, her cheeks turning pink.*

'Just introduce me,' he said.

'If you like,' John said. 'Just be careful, my friend. Girls like her can be lethal to men like you and you know it.'

Hayden couldn't answer that. When was he ever careful? He wasn't about to start now, not when feelings were roiling through him he had never felt before. He set off across the crowded room, leaving John to scramble after him.

And Miss Bancroft watched him approach. She still looked so very still, but he saw her gloved fingers tighten on the sticks of her fan, saw her sudden intake of breath against the satin of her bodice. She wasn't indifferent to him. Whatever this strange, sudden spell was, he wasn't in it alone.

'Miss Bancroft,' John said, giving the girl a bow. 'Very nice to see you again.'

'And you, Lord John,' she answered, her voice low and soft, musical, with a flash of gentle humour in its depths. 'It is a most du-

tiful brother who would brave a Drawing Room for his sister.'

John laughed and half-turned. 'May I present my very good friend, Hayden Fitzwalter, the Earl of Ramsay? He especially asked to make your acquaintance. Hayden, this is Miss Jane Bancroft.'

'How do you do?' she murmured. She made a little curtsy and slowly held out her hand to him.

Her fingers trembled a bit as he folded them in his own, and her cheeks turned a deeper pink. Jane, Jane.

And in that moment he was utterly lost...

Curiosus Semper.

Careful Always. Jane had to laugh as she tore a trailing veil of ivy away from the stone garden bench and saw the motto carved there. The letters were faded with time, encrusted with the moss and dirt of neglect, but they were still visible. She would wager her ancestors never could have foreseen how sadly ironic those words would be for their family.

She stood up and dusted some of the soil

and leaves from her gloved hands. Her shoulders ached from kneeling there, clearing away some of the tenaciously clinging vines, but it was a good ache. Work meant she didn't have to think. And there was plenty of work to be done at Barton Park.

As she stretched, she studied the house that loomed across the garden. Barton Park had belonged to the Bancrofts for centuries, a gift to one of their ancestors from Charles II. Legend had it that the house was part of the payment in exchange for that long-ago Bancroft marrying one of the king's many cast-off mistresses. But the marriage, against all odds, was a happy one, and the couple went on to make Barton Park a centre of raucous parties and all sorts of debauchery.

Just the sort of place Hayden would have liked, Jane often thought. Perhaps if she had been more like that first mistress of Barton Park things between them could have worked out. But the Bancrofts that followed were quieter, more scholarly, and not as adept at accumulating royal gifts. Their fortune dwindled until by the time of Jane's father there was little left but the house itself, which was already crumbling with neglect.

Little but the legend of the treasure. The old tale about how one of the first Barton Park Bancrofts' many licentious guests had dabbled in highway robbery and had hidden his ill-gotten treasure somewhere in the garden. Jane's father, as he grew sicker and sicker, had become obsessed with the idea of this treasure. He told Jane the story of it over and over, even sending her out to try digging in various spots around the grounds.

Then he died and her mother had told her different tales. Harder, more bitter stories about the truth of a woman's insecure place in the world, of how finding the right husband—a *rich* husband—was all that mattered. Jane was frightened to think she might be right. Money and position could bring security, of course, and she craved that so much after the uncertainties of her childhood. But surely there must be more? Must be some chance of a happy family? Of being a good wife and mother, despite the poor example she had always seen before her.

Then her mother also died and Jane went

to have a London Season with her aunt while Emma was sent to school.

Both those destinations had ended badly for the Bancroft sisters. Jane had found she had more of her fanciful father in her than she ever would have thought. She had imagined she had found a fairy tale, a happy-ever-after with Hayden, until she discovered she was in love with an illusion, a man who never really existed except in her dreams. She didn't know how to fit into his world and he couldn't help her. They had been so young, so foolish to think that they could even try, that their passion in the bedroom could be enough to make a life together.

So her father had been wrong in relying on fairy stories. But so had her mother. A rich husband was not all a woman needed.

Jane tossed her trowel and garden gloves into a bucket and examined the house. Barton Park was not a large dwelling, but once it had been very pretty, a red brick faded to a soft pink, centred around a white-stone portico and surrounded by gardens, a mysterious hedge maze and a pretty Chinoiserie summerhouse. Now the stone was chipped, some of the windows cracked and the lovely gardens sadly overgrown. She hadn't gone in the hedge maze at all since she moved back.

Jane did her best. She and Emma lived on a small bequest from their mother's family, which Hayden could probably claim if he wanted, but it was surely too insignificant to interest him. It paid for their food, a cook, a maid, fuel for the fires, but not a carriage or a team of gardeners. No grand parties, but she had had her fill of those in London. She had found she wasn't at all good at them, either attending or hosting them. There could be money from Hayden, but she couldn't bring herself to touch it.

Jane sighed as she pushed the loose tendrils of her brown hair back into her scarf. Emma was sixteen now. In a couple of years she should have a London Season, though Jane had no idea how to pay for it or how to weather London gossip in order to launch her.

Not that Emma seemed in the least bit interested in a Season. She was a strange girl, always buried in books about botany or running off to the woods to collect 'specimens' or bring home new pets like rabbits or hedge-hogs. She liked the quiet life in the country as much as Jane did. They both needed its peace. But Jane knew it couldn't go on for ever.

That was why she had forced herself to write to Hayden after all these years. It had taken days of agonising before she could take up that pen to write the letter and even more before she could send it. Then there was…

Nothing. The days had gone by in silence with no answer at all from her husband.

Her husband. Jane pressed her hand to her stomach with the spasm of pain that always came when she thought those words. She remembered Hayden as she had last seen him, sprawled asleep on the stairs of their London house. Her husband, as beautiful as a fallen angel. How horribly they had disappointed each other. Failed each other.

She tried so hard not to think about him. Not to think about how things were when they first married, when she had been so naïve and full of hope. So dazzled by Hayden and what he gave to her. By who he was and the delights they found together in the bedchamber. She tried not to think about the babies, and about how losing those tiny, fragile lives showed her how hollow and empty everything was. She couldn't even fulfil her main duty as a countess.

During the day it was easy not to think about it all. There was so much work to be done, the gardens to be cleared, the meagre accounts to go over, a few neighbourhood friends to call on or join for tea or cards. But at night—at night it was so different.

In the silence and the darkness there was nothing but the memories. She remembered everything about their days together, the good and the bad. How they had laughed together; how he had made her feel when he kissed her, touched her. How in those moments she had felt not so alone any longer, even though it was all an illusion in the end. She wondered how he was now, what he was doing. And then she wanted to sob for what was lost, for what had never really been except in her dreams.

Yes. Except for those nights, life would be very tolerable indeed. But it wasn't just Emma's future she needed to think about, it was her own. And Hayden's, too, even though the future had never seemed to be something he considered. He was an earl and also an orphan with no siblings. He would need an heir. And for that he would have to be free, as complicated and costly as that would be. She had to offer him that.

And she needed to be free, too.

Jane pushed away thoughts of Hayden and the unanswered letter. She couldn't worry about it now. She scooped up the bucket and made her way along the overgrown pathway to the house. They were expecting guests for tea.

As she stowed the bucket next to the kitchen, the door suddenly flew open and Emma dashed out. She held a wriggling puppy under one arm and the dirty burlap bag she used for collecting plants over the other. Her golden-blonde hair was gathered in an untidy braid and she wore an old apron over her faded blue-muslin dress.

Even so dishevelled, anyone could see that Emma was becoming a rare beauty, all ivory and gold with their mother's jewel-green eyes, eyes that had become a muddy hazel on Jane. Emma's beauty was yet another reason to worry about the future. Emma might be happy at Barton Park, but Jane knew she couldn't be buried in the country for ever.

'Where are you going in such a hurry?' Jane asked.

'I saw a patch of what looked like the plant I've been seeking by the road yesterday, but I didn't have time to examine it properly,' Emma answered briskly. 'I want to collect a few pieces before they get trampled.'

'It looks like rain,' Jane said. 'And we have guests coming to tea soon.'

'Do we? Who? The vicar again?' Emma said without much interest. She put down Murray the puppy and clipped on his lead.

'No, Sir David Marton and his sister Miss Louisa. Surely you remember them from the assembly last month?' Their last real social outing, dancing and tepid punch at the village assembly rooms. Emma would surely remember it as she had protested being put into one of Jane's made-over London gowns and had then been ogled and flirted with by every man between fifteen and fifty. Sir

David had danced with her once, too, then he had spent the evening talking to Jane.

'That old stick-in-the-mud?' Emma said with a scoffing laugh. 'What is he going to do, read us sermons?'

'Emma!' Jane protested. 'Sir David is hardly old—I doubt he is even thirty. And he is not in the least bit sermon-like. He and his sister are very nice.'

'Nice enough, I suppose, but still very stick-in-the-muddy. When he danced with me at the assembly he kept going on about some German philosopher with terribly gloomy ideas. He didn't know anything about botany. And his sister only seemed to care about hats.'

'Nevertheless, they *are* nice, and they are to be our nearest neighbours since they took over Easton Abbey,' Jane said, trying not to laugh at her sister's idea of proper social discourse. 'You need to be here when they call. And properly dressed, not drenched from getting caught in the rain.'

'I won't be gone long at all, Jane, I promise,' Emma said. 'I will be all prim and proper in the sitting room when they get here, ready to talk about German philosophy over cakes and tea.'

Jane laughed as Emma kissed her cheek and hurried away, Murray barking madly at her feet. 'Half an hour, Emma, no more.'

'Half an hour! I promise!'

Once Emma was gone out the garden gate, Jane hurried through the kitchens, where their cook was making a rare fine tea of sandwiches and lemon cakes, and went up the back stairs to her chamber. Emma wasn't the only one who needed to mend her appearance, she thought as she caught a glimpse of herself in the dressing-table mirror. She could pass as the scullery maid herself.

And somehow it seemed so important that Sir David and his sister not think ill of her appearance.

As she tugged the scarf from her hair and untied her apron, she thought about Sir David and their recent meetings. He was a handsome young man, in a quiet way that matched his polite demeanour. With his sandy-brown hair and spectacles, he seemed to exude an unobtrusive intelligence that Jane found calming after all that had happened before in her life.

She enjoyed talking to him and he seemed to enjoy talking to her. When she had declined to dance at the assembly, saying only that her dancing days were behind her, he did not press her. But he was kind enough to dance with Emma and listen to her talk about plants, even though Emma seemed to find him 'stick-in-the-muddy'.

So when Jane had encountered him and his sister in the village, it seemed natural to invite them to tea. Only to be a friendly neighbour, of course. There could be nothing more. She was a married woman, even though she had not seen her husband in years.

She was a married woman for now, anyway. And she could not quite deny that when David Marton smiled at her, sought her out for conversation, she felt something she hadn't in a long time. She felt—admired.

Even before she left London she had begun to feel invisible. The one person whose admiration mattered—her husband—didn't see her any more and all the chatter in the fashion papers about her gowns and her coiffures didn't matter at all. Nothing mattered beyond Hayden's indifference. She started to feel invisible even to herself, especially after she had failed in her main duty to give her husband an heir.

Back home at Barton Park she had started to feel better, slowly, day by day. She had started to feel the sun on her skin again and hear the birds singing. The weed-choked gardens didn't care what she looked like and Emma certainly didn't. Things seemed quite content. So it had come as quite a surprise how much she enjoyed Sir David's quiet attentions.

She leaned towards the mirror to peer more closely at her reflection.

'No one in London would recognise you now,' she said with laugh. And, indeed, no one *would* recognise the well-dressed Lady Ramsay in this woman, with her wind-tossed hair and the pale gold freckles the sun had dotted over her nose. She reached for her hairbrush and set to work.

She suddenly felt giddily schoolgirlish in how much she looked forward to this tea party.

Chapter Three

'Ramsay? By Jove, it *is* you! Blast it, man, what are you doing in this godforsaken place?'

Hayden slowly turned from his place at the bar. He had just been asking himself that very thing. What was he doing in a country inn, sipping at tepid, weak ale, running after a woman who clearly didn't want him, when he could be in London, getting ready for a night out at balls and gambling clubs?

He had just come to the startling realisation that a night out gaming and drinking wasn't something he would miss very much when he heard those shouted words. They were a welcome distraction from his own brooding thoughts.

He turned away from the bar and saw Lord Ethan Carstairs making his way across the crowded room towards him. Lord Ethan was not what Hayden would call a friend, but they were often in the same circles and saw each other at their club and across the gambling tables. Lord Ethan was rather loud and didn't hold his liquor very well, but he was tolerable enough most of the time. Especially at moments like this, when Hayden needed distraction.

'Lord Ethan,' he said. 'Fancy seeing you here. Can I buy you an ale?'

'I won't say no to that,' Ethan said affably as he leaned against the bar next to Hayden. To judge by his reddened cheeks and rumpled hair, and the dishevelled state of his expensive clothes, he had been imbibing the ale for quite a while already. 'My damnable uncle is making me rusticate for a while. Says he won't increase my allowance until I learn some control and I am completely out of funds.'

'Indeed?' Hayden asked without much

interest as he gestured to the innkeeper for more ale. Everyone knew that Ethan's Puritanical uncle, who also held the Carstairs family purse-strings, disapproved of his nephew's wild ways. Hayden sympathised. His own father had so often been disapproving.

And now here he was, drowning his doubts in drink. Just like his father. That was certainly something he did *not* want to think about.

'Most unfair,' Ethan grumbled. He took a long gulp from his glass, the reached into his pocket and took out a small, gold object he twirled through his fingers. Hayden recognised it as an old Spanish coin the man often used as a lucky charm at the card tables. 'I'm on my way to some country pile to wait him out. But what are *you* doing so far from town?'

Hayden shrugged. He might as well tell the truth. All of society would know soon enough, when he either came back to London with Jane by his side or instigated scandalous divorce proceedings. 'I am on my way to Barton Park to see Lady Ramsay.'

'By Jove!' Ethan sputtered. 'I had forgotten you were married.'

'My wife is delicate and prefers the country for her health,' Hayden said, as he always did when someone asked about Jane. They seldom even bothered any longer.

'I see. I remember they said she was a pretty little thing.' Ethan's gaze narrowed, and for an instant it was as if the ale-haze cleared in his bloodshot-blue eyes. 'Barton Park, you say?'

'It's her family home.'

'I think I have heard of it. Isn't there some tale of treasure or some such there?' Ethan laughed, and that instant of clarity vanished. 'We can both rot here in the country for a while, then. Damnable families.'

Damnable families. Hayden almost laughed bitterly as he sipped at the terrible ale. He wasn't even sure what it felt like to have a family, not now. He had been alone for so long it seemed like the only way he could be. The only way he could avoid hurting anyone else.

Once, for a moment, he had seen what it could be to have a real family. He had a flashing memory of a sunlit day, of Jane with her dark hair loose over her bare shoulders, smiling up at him. She took his hand and held it against the warm skin of her stomach, where he could feel the swell of their child. The first child that was lost.

He knew now that that was the most perfect moment of his life, but it had only been an illusion. Jane was done with him now. But he wasn't done with her. Soon enough she would see that.

'I have to be on my way,' Hayden said. He pushed his half-full glass away. 'Good luck with your rusticating, Carstairs.'

Lord Ethan blinked at him. 'Same to you, Ramsay. Maybe we'll meet again soon.'

Hayden nodded, though really he was quite sure they wouldn't. He left the stale-smelling room behind for the innyard. As he waited for a fresh horse to be brought around, one of the servants said, 'It looks like rain is coming, my lord. Might be best to wait to ride out.'

Hayden peered up at the sky. It had been a pale blue when he arrived at the inn, hazy with country sunlight, but now he saw the servant was right. Grey clouds were gathering swiftly and the wind was colder.

But the thought of going back inside to drink some more with Ethan Carstairs was most unappealing. He had already waited too long to go after Jane—he needed to get on with the business of confronting his wife.

'I haven't far to ride,' he said as he swung up into the saddle. But he hadn't been gone long from the inn when the lowering skies burst open on a clap of thunder and rain poured down.

Hayden was glad of the cold, it seemed to drive him onwards and cleared his head. He galloped faster down the narrow, rutted lane, revelling in the speed and the wildness of the nature around him. All too often in London he felt closed in, trapped by the buildings and the noise, by all the people watching him.

Here there was nothing but the trees and the wind, the dark clouds sweeping in faster and faster over his head on the rumble of thunder. Maybe that was why Jane had run here, he thought as his horse leaped over a fallen log in the road and galloped onwards even faster. Just to be able to breathe again.

He urged the horse on, trying to outrun the raw anger that had burned in him ever since he had read Jane's letter. Even if she was tired of her London life, she had duties, damn it! Duties as his wife and countess. She had left them, left him, behind. And now she wanted to abandon them permanently.

She had to see how impossible her suggestion of divorce was. He had to *make* her see.

A bolt of sizzling blue-white lightning suddenly split the sky, cleaving a tree beside the road only a few feet away. With a deafening crack, a thick branch split away and crashed into the road. Hayden's horse reared up and the wet reins slid from his hands at the sudden movement.

He felt himself falling, the sky and the rain and the mud all tumbling around him. He crashed to the ground and pain shot through his leg as it twisted under him.

Hayden cursed as loudly as he could, but he was drowned out by the shout of the thunder. The horse scrambled to regain his footing and ran away down the lane. Hayden tried to push himself up, to balance on his good leg, but he fell back to the mud.

He shoved back his sodden hair and stared up into the leaden sky. He laughed at the storm. It seemed even nature wanted to keep him away from Jane.

'Are you all right?' he heard a woman call. He twisted around to see her running towards him through the misty sheets of rain, like a ghost.

She looked vaguely familiar, not very tall and too slender in a faded, rain-spotted dress. A loose braid of wet golden hair lay over her shoulder and a barking puppy ran in circles around her. But despite that nagging sense that he should know her, he didn't really recognise her as she ran down the lane towards him.

Until she knelt beside him, completely careless of the rain. She stared up at him with bright green eyes, pale and clear. He remembered those eyes. He had seen them at his wedding when Jane proudly introduced her sister. She had been younger then, scrawny and awkward. Now time had moved on and she had grown up.

And he remembered that Jane had written

that her sister lived with her now. He had to be close to Barton Park.

'Emma?' he said.

She sat back on her heels, her eyes narrowing with suspicion. 'Yes, I am Emma Bancroft. How do you…?' Suddenly she gasped. 'Ramsay? What in the hell are you doing here?'

'Does your sister let you curse like that? Most unladylike,' he said, suddenly aware of the utter absurdity of his situation. He was sitting in the rain, in the middle of a muddy country lane, arguing about propriety with the sister-in-law he hardly knew.

He laughed and she frowned at him as if he was an escaped bedlamite. He certainly felt like one.

'Of course she doesn't let me,' Emma said. 'But she is not here and this situation clearly warrants a curse or two. What are *you* doing here? Aren't you supposed to be in London?'

'I was, but now I'm on my way to Barton Park. Or I was, until that infernal horse threw me.'

Emma glanced over her shoulder at where

the horse had come to a halt further down the lane. 'Are you hurt?'

'I think I twisted my leg. I can't stand up.'

Her frown of suspicion vanished, replaced by an expression of concern. Perhaps like her sister she was too soft-hearted. 'Oh, no! Here, let me help you.'

'I'm far too heavy for you.'

'Nonsense. I'm much stronger than I look.' She wrapped her arm around him and let him lean on her as he staggered to his feet. She *was* rather strong, and between them they managed to hobble over to the fallen branch.

'Stay here, Ramsay, and I'll get your horse back,' she said. 'You need to get out of the rain and have that leg looked at.'

She dashed away, leaving her now-silent dog to watch him suspiciously in her place. She returned very quickly with the recalcitrant horse.

'We aren't far from Barton Park,' she said. 'I can lead you there, if you can manage to ride that far.'

'Of course I can ride that far, it's just a sprain,' he said, even though his leg felt like it was on fire and he could see blood spotting his rain-soaked breeches.

'Good. You'll need to save your strength for when Jane sees you. She doesn't know you're coming, does she?' Emma asked matter of factly, as if she ran into estranged relatives every day.

Hayden gritted his teeth as he pulled himself up into the saddle. The pain washed over him in cold waves and he pushed it away. 'Not yet.'

To his surprise, Emma laughed. 'Oh, this day just gets more interesting all the time.'

Emma tried not to stare at her brother-in-law like a lackwit, tried to just calmly give him directions to Barton Park as he pulled her up on to the horse behind him and set them into motion, Murray running alongside them. But she just couldn't help it. She couldn't believe Lord Ramsay was actually there, that she had actually stumbled on him right in the middle of the road as she tried to hurry home for tea.

Whatever was he doing there? It couldn't possibly be good. As far as Emma knew,

Jane hadn't even talked to him in all the time since they came to live at Barton. Jane never even talked *about* him, so Emma had no idea what had happened in London.

But she did have imagination and it had filled in all sorts of lurid scenarios that could drive her kind-hearted, responsible sister away from her husband. Ramsay had become something of an ogre in Emma's mind, so her first instinct when she saw him there in the road had been to run from him as fast as she could. Especially after what had happened to her at school, with that odious Mr Milne, the music master. He had been enough to scare her off men for ever.

And yet—yet she remembered that one other time she had met Ramsay, on the day he married her sister in that elegant town ceremony. He had looked at Jane then as if all the stars and the moon revolved only around her and he had held her hand so tenderly. And Jane had been radiant that day, as if she was lit from within. Emma had never seen her sister, who tended to worry over everyone else so much, so very happy. Emma had even known she could endure her hated school because she knew Jane was happy in her new life with her husband.

What had gone so wrong? Why was Ramsay here now, after so long? Emma was bursting to know, but she just said calmly, 'Turn right up there at the gate.'

'Thank you, Miss Bancroft,' he said through gritted teeth. When she glanced up at his profile, she saw he looked rather pale. He was probably in more pain than he wanted to show, just like a man.

'I hardly think we need to be so formal,' she said teasingly. 'I'm your sister. My name is Emma.'

A flash of a smile touched his lips. 'I do remember your name, Emma.'

'That's good. If you turn left here, you'll see the house just ahead.'

'Thank you,' he said again. 'So, Emma, what are you doing running about in the rain?'

'It wasn't raining when I left,' she said. 'And if you must know, I was collecting some specimens.'

'Specimens?'

'Plants. For my studies.' And she really

had taken a few cuttings of the plants. He didn't need to know her other errands. No one had to know, not yet, that she was hunting for the lost Barton Park treasure.

Emma tucked her sack closer to her side and felt the reassuring weight of the small journal in its pocket. She had found it in a forgotten corner of the Barton library last month. She had been hoping to find old plans of the gardens, but this book was even better. It was a journal belonging to the young cousin of the first mistress of Barton Park.

It seemed this girl had been a poor relation, sent to stay at Barton to gain some Court polish. Emma didn't know her name, but she had quickly been drawn into her sharply observed tales of the people and parties of the house back then. Barton was so quiet now, silently crumbling away with only her and Jane living there, but once upon a time it had been full of life and scandal.

Then the journal's writer had fallen in love with one of the naughty guests—the very man who had stolen the treasure and hid it somewhere in the gardens. Emma had been combing its yellowed pages for clues ever since.

Surely if she could find it, their worries would be over. Jane could cease working so very hard, could lose that pinched, concerned look on her face. Jane had always been the best of sisters. Emma only wanted to help her, too.

But she didn't want Jane to know what she was doing. Emma didn't want to be compared to their father, so caught up in useless dreams he couldn't help his family. So she did her detective work in secret, whenever she could. And she had found nothing yet.

She had also never told her sister about what had really happened at school with Mr Milne. That was only for her nightmares now, thankfully. She was done with men altogether.

'There's the house,' she said. It loomed before them in the misty rain and she was glad he couldn't yet see the dwelling clearly. Couldn't see how shabby it was. If only she had had time to warn Jane! Then again, maybe the surprise was better.

But if she had vague hopes that Ramsay's

leg would slow him down enough to give her a head start into the house, they were quickly dashed. He held on to his saddle and carefully slid to the ground, his jaw set in his handsome, hard-edged face.

Emma leaped down and ran up the front steps to throw the door open. Murray dashed in, barking, his muddy paw prints trailing over the old, scarred parquet floor.

'Jane, Jane!' she shouted, completely abandoning propriety. She had only seconds to warn her sister. Then she could watch the drama unfold.

Jane emerged from the drawing-room door, her eyes wide with astonishment. She had changed from her garden clothes to her best day dress, a pale green muslin with a high-frilled collar. Her brown hair was carefully pinned up and bound with a green-ribbon bandeau. For a second, Emma couldn't decipher why her sister was so dressed up on a rainy afternoon.

Then the Martons, Sir David and his silly sister, appeared in the doorway behind her and Emma remembered in a flash. They had guests. *Respectable* guests, who for some unfathomable reason Jane wanted to impress.

'Emma, whatever is the matter?' Jane demanded, while Sir David looked rather disapproving and his sister giggled behind her handkerchief.

'He is here!' Emma cried. She couldn't worry about the Martons right now, not with Ramsay so close behind her.

'Who is here?' Jane said. 'Emma, dear, are you ill?'

Across the empty hall, the door opened again, letting in a blast of rain and wind. Ramsay stood there, silhouetted in his greatcoat against the grey sky outside. For one instant there was a flash of something raw and burning, something real, in his eyes. Then it was as if a blank, pale mask dropped down and there was nothing at all.

'Hello, Jane,' he said calmly. 'It's been much too long. You are looking lovely as always.'

Emma swung back around to look at Jane. Her sister's face had turned utterly white and Emma feared she might faint right in front of everyone. But when Emma moved to take her hand, Jane waved her back.

'Oh, blast it all,' Jane whispered. 'Not now...'

'You can't feel it move yet,' Jane said, her voice full of laughter. 'It's much too soon.'

Hayden laid down beside her on the sun-splashed bed anyway and rested his cheek on the gentle swell of her belly under her light dressing gown. It was early; the doctor had only just confirmed that Jane was truly pregnant. But his wife already seemed blooming. She wasn't quite as thin and her cheeks were pink. Four months married and now a child on the way. Their first child.

She laughed again as he carefully touched the small bump. Her skin was so warm, so sweet, so alive. 'You won't break me, Hayden. The doctor says I am quite healthy.'

Hayden fervently prayed so. He didn't know what he had ever done in his misbegotten life to deserve a wife like Jane, but he knew he couldn't lose her now. His heart ached just to think of her laughter, her quite, calm presence, being gone in a flash.

Just like his mother.

Jane seemed to sense his sudden fear. She gently smoothed a soft caress over his hair. 'All will be well, Hayden. I am sure of it. And in a few months, we will have a little lord or lady. The beginning of a new family for us. Just like we talked about on our honeymoon.'

Their honeymoon—those perfect, sweet days and nights, just the two of them all alone in the country. They had almost become buried under the noise and rush of London life since they returned. Jane had seemed a bit lost as a new countess, with so many eyes upon her, but now she looked perfectly content. A new family was on the way, their family. It could be very different from what he knew with his parents. He could make it different.

But still the tiny, buried spark of that old fear lingered...

Chapter Four

'Won't you introduce me to your guests?'

Hayden. Hayden was here, standing in her house. Jane was sure she must have fallen and hit her head, that she was lying on the drawing-room floor having dream visions. One minute she was serving tea, trying to make polite conversation as she worried about Emma wandering around out in the rain. And the next she was facing her husband.

Her husband. It truly was Hayden, after all these years. She stared at him, frozen, stricken. Her dreams of him had been nothing to the real thing. Hayden was even more handsome than she remembered, his elegantly sharp-planed face drawn even leaner, harsher with his black hair slicked back with the rain.

His eyes, that pure, pale blue she had once so loved, stared back at her unwavering. For an instant she went tumbling back to that moment when she first saw him. She was that romantic girl again, hopeful, heartstruck, so sure that she saw her own passionate need reflected in those eyes. So sure he was what she had been longing for all her life. Hayden, Hayden—he was here again!

She almost took a step towards him, almost reached for him, when he suddenly smiled at her. But it was not a smile of joyful welcome. It was sardonic, almost bitter, the smile of a sophisticated stranger. It made Jane remember what had become of her romantic dreams of marriage and the man she had thought was her husband. He had been living his fast life in London while she was healing here in the country. Hayden was truly only a stranger now.

Jane's half-lifted hand fell back to her side and the haze of dreams cleared around her. For a moment she had seen only Hayden, but suddenly she was aware of everything else. The rain pounding at the windows. Emma beside her, her golden hair dripping on to the floor, watching her with a frown of concern. The Martons just behind, witnessing this whole bizarre tableau of unexpected reunion.

The way that Hayden leaned heavily on the wobbly old pier table. There was a tear in his finely tailored breeches and spots of blood on the pale fabric muted by the rainwater.

Jane's throat tightened at the realisation that he was hurt. 'What has happened?' she asked hoarsely.

It was Emma who answered. 'I found him on the road,' she said. 'His horse had thrown him and his leg was so hurt he couldn't stand.'

'Thrown him?' Jane said. Surely that was impossible. Hayden was one of the finest riders she knew. Despite her fears and doubts, she couldn't help but be concerned he was truly hurt.

'A lightning strike startled the horse,' he said, remarkably calm for a man who was standing drenched and wounded in his estranged wife's house. 'I fear I'm interrupting a social occasion.'

'I— No, not at all,' Jane managed to choke out. 'Merely tea with our neighbours. This is Sir David Marton and his sister, Miss Louisa Marton. May I present Lord Ramsay, my— my husband.'

'Your husband?' Miss Louisa cried. 'Why, how very exciting. We were not expecting to meet you here, my lord.'

'No, I imagine not,' Hayden murmured. 'How do you do?'

Miss Louisa giggled while Sir David said nothing. Jane sensed him watching her, but she couldn't deal with him now. She had to take care of Hayden. She forced herself to move, to go across the hall and reach for Hayden's arm.

For an instant he was stiff under her tentative touch and she thought he would jerk away from her. But he let her thread her fingers around his elbow and swayed towards her.

Up close, she could see how carefully rigid he held his body, the bruised-looking shadows under his eyes. He felt thinner, harder than he had the last time she had touched him. But his smell was the same, that clean, crisp scent of sun and lemony cologne and man that had once made her long to curl up beside him and inhale him into her very heart. There was the faint undertone of ale, but the brandy was gone.

'We need to get you upstairs and send for the doctor,' Jane said quietly. He was obviously in more pain than he would ever reveal.

'I can go,' Emma said.

'No, permit me to go for the doctor, Lady Ramsay,' Sir David said. 'Louisa and I have the carriage and Miss Bancroft should be by the fire.'

Jane glanced over at Sir David, surprised by the offer. He didn't smile, just looked back at her solemnly and gave her a polite nod. The tea had been going rather well, she suddenly remembered, until this most unexpected interruption. Unlike Emma, Jane rather enjoyed hearing about philosophy, books and ideas, and Sir David was an intelligent, pleasant conversationalist. He had seemed to enjoy talking to her as well, and if nothing else his company gave her hope that life would not always be so lonely. That life could be—nice, rather than chaotic or painful.

Then Hayden appeared.

'Thank you, Sir David,' she said. 'That is so kind of you.' He nodded and took his sister's arm to lead her away. She waved at them merrily over her shoulder.

Emma tactfully withdrew, leaving Jane alone with Hayden for the first time in three years. Jane took a deep, steadying breath. She had to help him just as she would anyone else who showed up on her doorstep in a storm. He was merely a stranger to her now.

But he didn't *feel* like a stranger as she took his arm again. His eyes weren't those of a stranger as he looked down at her. Once he had known her so well, better than anyone else ever had. He had known her body as well as the secrets of her heart. She had trusted him so much, allowed him to see so much.

She had bitterly regretted that ever since. She could never let herself be so vulnerable again.

She turned away from the blue light of his eyes. 'Let me help you up the stairs,' she said softly.

'Do you have no butler or footmen?' Hayden asked. 'Those stairs look rather precarious.'

Jane almost laughed. 'We have an elderly cook and a shy little maid who is no doubt cowering in the pantry right now. I'm the only help available, I fear.'

Hayden nodded grimly and let her hold on to his arm as she led him slowly up the stairs. She sensed he was trying to lean on her as little as possible, even as his jaw was set with the pain. She never really noticed the staircase any longer, it was always just *there*. But now she saw it through his eyes, the missing carved posts, the chips in the once-gilded balustrade, the loose boards in the risers.

'I usually use the back stairs,' she said. 'But they are rather a long walk from here.'

Hayden nodded again and together they concentrated on getting to the landing. At the top, they faced the long corridor lined with closed doors and Jane realised there was

no choice. She had to take him to her room.
Besides Emma's, none of the other chambers
were habitable.

She pushed open the door and led him over
to the old *chaise* next to the window. He lowered himself down to its faded cushions, still
looking up at her with those eyes that seemed
to see so much. Seemed to remember her,
know her.

Jane remembered that when he was drinking, when he was caught up in his London
life, he didn't seem to see her at all. Why was
he here, now, finally looking at her when she
had at last gained a small measure of contentment?

*'What do you want, Jane? What in God's
name will make you happy? You have everything here.'*

Those long-ago words of Hayden's suddenly rang in her memory. The frustration
in them, the anger. And she remembered her
own tears.

*'All I want is for you to spend time with
me,'* she answered, so confused that he
couldn't understand without her saying anything. *That he didn't* know.

'I was with you all last night, Jane.'

'At a ball.' A ball where they had danced once and then he had disappeared into the card room. He had not even made love to her when they got home near dawn. And the times when they had made love, when it was only the two of them alone in the darkness, were the only times she felt sure he was really with her.

'Let's go back to Ramsay House, like on our honeymoon,' she had begged, trying not to cry again. She was so tired of crying. 'We had such fun there.'

'We have duties here, Jane. Don't be ridiculous.'

'Duties!' And that was when anger overtook the hurt confusion inside of her. 'Duties to do what? Go to the races with your friends? Play cards? You are surely needed at your estate.' Needed by her. *But she dared not say that again.*

'You don't understand,' he had answered coldly. 'You are new to being a countess. But you will learn.'

Only she never had learned how to be the sort of countess he wanted. A woman at ease in the racy environs of society. A woman who could give him an heir. A woman his friends would admire. She gave up even trying, especially after she lost the babies.

'You should change out of your wet clothes,' she said. 'I'll see if I can find something in my father's old wardrobe.'

She turned away, but Hayden suddenly reached out and caught her hand in his. His fingers were cool and strong as they twined with hers, holding her with him. It felt strange, new and wonderfully familiar all at the same time. She stared down at him, startled.

A smile touched his sensual lips, an echo of that bright, rakish grin that once drew her in so completely.

'Will you not help me out of my wet clothes, Jane?' he said. 'You used to be so good at that...'

Jane snatched her hand away. 'I'm glad the fall didn't damage *everything,* Hayden. You can take them off all by yourself, I'm sure.'

More flustered than she would ever admit, Jane whirled around and hurried towards the door.

'Jane,' he called.

She stopped with her hand on the latch. 'Yes? What now?'

'Who was your visitor?'

His tone had flashed from teasing and suggestive to hard, demanding. As if he had any right to demand anything of her any longer!

She glanced back at him over her shoulder. The stark grey light from the window surrounded him, blinding her. 'I told you, the Martons are our neighbours. We were having tea.'

'Is that all?' he said. He sounded ridiculously suspicious.

'Of course,' Jane snapped, suddenly angry. He knew nothing of her life at Barton Park, just as she knew nothing now of his London life. She didn't *want* to know; she could imagine it all too well. And she was sure he did nothing so innocent as take tea and talk about books with his neighbours.

'What are you even doing here, Hayden?' she said. 'Why now?'

Hayden shook his head and, as Jane blinked away that unwelcome prickle of tears, she saw how weary he looked. He slumped back on to the *chaise* and she knew this was not the moment for any long-delayed quarrels and confrontations. Those could wait.

'I will fetch some dry clothes and some water for you to wash,' she said and slipped out the door.

Once alone in the dark corridor, she leaned against the wall and impatiently rubbed at her aching eyes. She had already cried enough tears over Hayden; she wouldn't shed any more. She would find out what he wanted then send him on his way so she could resume her life without him.

That was her only choice now.

The door closed behind the doctor and Hayden let his head fall back on to the worn cushions of the *chaise* and closed his eyes. His whole body felt as if he had gone three rounds at Gentleman Jackson's Saloon and then got foxed and fallen off his horse on top of that. He felt battered, bruised and exhausted, and his leg burned fiercely, especially after all the doctor's poking and prodding.

But the pain of his leg was nothing to the

pain of seeing Jane again. He wasn't expecting the bolt of pure, hot longing that would hit him just from seeing her face. Touching her, feeling her nearness. He had thought he had forgotten about her in the busy noise of his life, that their separation was nothing. That he didn't miss her. That she was just a distant acquaintance.

But then she stepped out of the doorway and the sight of her face hit him like another lightning strike, sudden and paralysing. Almost like the first time he saw her and couldn't turn away from the light of her shy smile. Couldn't turn away from the hope she kindled inside him.

In that moment before she saw him, she had looked concerned about her sister, her hazel-green eyes soft with worry. Until she glimpsed him and they froze over like a spring tree branch in a sudden frost. Her slender shoulders had stiffened and he had the feeling that she would have fled if all her weighty good manners and pride hadn't held her there.

Jane always had exquisite manners, was always concerned about the people around her. Including those blasted visitors today? What was their name—Marton? Yes, that Marton was too good looking, too polished and perfect and serious. Damn him. Somehow Hayden had imagined Jane saw no one at all here in the country.

He shifted on the *chaise* and his leg sent out a stab of fresh pain in protest. There was the soft sound of voices outside the door, one of them the doctor's, stern and gravelly.

The other was Jane's, a gentle murmur, and its very softness hurt him even more. It made him think of the first time he came home drunk, after they returned to town from their long honeymoon at Ramsay House and he left Jane one night to go to the club with his friends. Those days alone with Jane had been so golden, so perfect and peaceful, unlike any he had ever known before in his life.

Then his friends had laughed about his new 'settled and domestic' ways, about how he would soon become one of those men who followed their wives about London like puppy dogs.

Hayden couldn't be that way, couldn't depend on anyone. Need anyone. He had seen how that had killed his parents. After his flighty, beautiful mother died in childbirth, his father couldn't bear it and followed her soon after. He had always vowed never to be like them. Yet he could see then how much he was coming to rely on Jane. That very night, his first night back at the club as a married man, he only wanted to leave his friends and go home to her. He couldn't have that. So he drank more than his fill of brandy to prove it.

Just as his father had always done.

And Jane had spoken to him softly that night as well. Had watched him with those concerned eyes as Makepeace helped him up the stairs.

'Not to worry, my lady,' Makepeace told her. 'This is merely what young men do in society.'

'But surely Ramsay does not...' she had said. Then she learned that Ramsay did and he saw that bright hope die in her eyes. He had killed it.

Hayden opened his eyes and found himself not a callow newlywed at his town house, but alone in a strange room with Jane's familiar voice outside. He studied the chamber for the first time since she brought him in there.

It wasn't a large room, but it was cosy and warm with thick blue curtains at the windows muffling the patter of the rain. There was the old *chaise*, a small inlaid desk piled with papers and ledgers, and a dressing table cluttered with pots and bottles and ribbons. The bed was an old one, dark, heavy carved wood spread with an embroidered coverlet. A dressing gown was tossed across its foot and a pair of slippers had been hastily kicked off on the faded rug beside it. A screen across the corner was also hung with clothes.

This had to be Jane's own room, Hayden realised with surprise. He recognised the silver hairbrush on the dressing table; he had run it through the silken strands of her hair several times, winding the long, soft length of it around his wrist. The smell of her lilac perfume still hung in the air.

He had forgotten what it was like to live with a lady, to be surrounded by cosy, feminine clutter. Why would she put him in here of all places?

The door opened and Jane herself appeared there. Emma peeked in behind her, her eyes wide with curiosity until Jane gently but firmly closed the door between them.

'The doctor said your leg is not broken, but the wound is a rather deep one. You'll have to stay still for a few days and let it heal,' she said. Her face was as still and smooth as a marble statue's, giving away nothing of her real thoughts.

Nothing about how she felt to have him in her home.

'Is this your own room, Jane?' he asked. His voice came out too rough, almost angry, and he felt immediately guilty when she flinched. He had never known quite how to behave around her—except in the bedchamber, when they knew how to be together only too well.

'Yes,' she said. She plucked up the silky dressing gown from the bed and stashed it behind the screen. 'I'm afraid we have few guests here at Barton, so only my room and Emma's are ready to be occupied. I can stay with her tonight and we'll tidy another chamber in the morning.'

'I can sleep in your drawing room,' he

said, forcing himself to be gentler, quieter. Jane's face was turned from him so he could see only her profile, that pure, serene, classical line of her nose and mouth he had always loved.

He suddenly longed to push back from the *chaise*, to grab her into his arms and pull her against him. To kiss her soft lips until she melted against him again and that ice that seemed to surround her melted. Until she was *his* Jane again.

But he knew he couldn't do that. The walls between them had been built too strong, too thick, brick by brick. He had done that himself. He had wanted it that way.

But he still wanted to kiss her.

'You're ill,' she said. 'I'm not helping you all the way downstairs again just so you can injure yourself once more.' She took a small bottle out of the pocket of the white apron she wore over her pretty green dress and put it down on the desk. 'The doctor left that to help you sleep. I'll bring you some water and something to eat. You must be hungry after your journey.'

'Jane,' Hayden called as she turned towards the door.

She glanced back at him over her shoulder, her hand poised on the latch. There was a flash of something, some emotion, deep in her hazel eyes, but it was gone before he could decipher it.

And he had forgotten what he wanted to say to her. No words could bridge this gap. 'Who is that man Marton?' he blurted.

Jane's lips twitched, but she didn't quite smile. 'Oh, Hayden. We can talk in the morning. The inn sent on your valise, I'll bring it up so you don't have to wear my father's shirt any longer.'

'Jane…' he shouted again, but she was gone as quickly and quietly as she had arrived. And he was alone with his thoughts, which was the very last place he ever wanted to be.

Chapter Five

Hayden was asleep.

Jane tiptoed carefully into the room and set her tray down as gently as possible on the dressing table. She didn't want to wake him. She had no idea what she would say to him. There were so many things she wanted to know. Why was he here? What did he want? Was he going to agree to a divorce?

And yet there was a part of her, a deep, fearful, secret part, that didn't want to know at all.

She eased back the edge of the window curtain to let in some morning light. Not that there was much of it. It still rained outside, a steady grey *drip-drip* against the windows

and the roof that she prayed wouldn't spring
a leak. Not now, with Hayden here. It was
bad enough he had seen Barton Park in all
its shabbiness.

She turned to study him as he slept on the
chaise. He hadn't moved to the bed, but was
stretched out under an old quilt on the *chaise*
where she had left him. The bottle of laudanum was untouched, yet he seemed to sleep
peacefully enough.

She tiptoed closer and studied him in the
watery grey light. It had been so long since
she saw him like this, so quiet and unaware,
so lost in dreams. She remembered when
they were first married, those bright honeymoon days at Ramsay House, when she
would lie there beside him every morning
and watch him as he slept. She would mar-
vel that he was *hers*, that they were together.

And then he would wake and smile at
her. He would reach for her, both of them
laughing as they rolled through the rumpled
sheets. It seemed like everything was just beginning for them then. What would she have
done if she knew that was all there would be?

Yesterday she had thought Hayden looked

different, like a hard, lean stranger dropped into her house. Yet right now he looked like *that* Hayden again, like the husband she had loved waking up with every morning. In sleep, the harsh lines of his face were smoothed and a small smile touched the corners of his lips as if he was having a good dream.

There were no arguments, no tears, no misunderstandings. Just Hayden.

Jane couldn't help herself. She knelt down by the *chaise* and reached out to carefully smooth a rumpled wave of black hair back from his brow. His skin was warm under her touch, but not feverish. She cupped her palm over his cheek and a wave of terrible tenderness washed over her. She hadn't realised until that moment just how much she had really missed Hayden.

Not the Hayden of London, the Hayden who had no time for his wife, but the man she had wanted so much to marry. How had that all fallen so very apart?

Suddenly his eyes opened, those glowing summer-blue eyes, and he stared up at her. His smile widened and she couldn't draw away from him—it was so very beautiful. His hand reached up to cover hers and hold her against him.

'Jane,' he said, his voice rough with sleep. 'I had the strangest dream…'

Then his gaze flickered past her to the room beyond and that smile vanished. That one magical instant, where the past was the present, was gone like a wisp of fog.

Jane pulled her hand away and pushed herself to her feet. She brushed her fingers over her apron, but she could still feel him on her skin. He rolled on to his back and groaned.

'How are you feeling this morning?' she said. She turned away and poured out a cup of tea on the tray.

'Like I was dragged backward by the heels through miles of hedgerow,' Hayden answered. He scowled at the cup she held out. 'Do you have anything stronger, perchance?'

She was definitely not giving him brandy. Not now, while she had the control. 'No, just tea. You didn't take the laudanum the doctor left?'

He shook his head and sipped cautiously at the tea when she held it out to him again.

'I had the feeling I would need a clear head today.'

'You should eat something, too, then I can change your bandage.' Jane gave him the plate of toast and sat down on the dressing-table bench. 'What are you doing here, Hayden?'

He chewed thoughtfully at a bite of the buttered bread before he set the plate aside. 'Because you wrote to me, of course.'

'But I never intended for you to come here!' Jane cried. 'You could have just written back to me.'

Hayden gave a humourless laugh. 'My wife demands a divorce and she thinks I should just write back a polite little letter? Saying what? "Oh, yes, Jane dear, whatever you want." It's not that simple.'

Jane closed her eyes tightly against the sight of Hayden sitting there in her bedchamber, so close, but so, so far. 'I know it's not simple at all. But surely we can't just go on as we have been for ever. You need a real wife, an heir. And this sham of a marriage—'

Hayden suddenly slammed his plate down on the floor. 'Our marriage is not a sham! We stood up in that church and made our vows before all of society. You are the Countess of Ramsay. My *wife*.'

Jane couldn't bear it any longer. He was right; when she walked down that aisle there had been nothing of the sham about it. She had wanted only to be his wife, to live her life with him. But nothing had turned out as she expected, nothing at all. And when the babies, their last hope, were gone...

'I have never really been your wife, have I?' she said, her voice thick with the tears she had held back for such a long time. 'We never wanted the same things, I was just too foolish to see that back then. We were so young and I didn't know what would happen.'

'What is it that you want, Jane? What have I not given you?' He sounded confused, hurt.

Yourself, she wanted to shout. But she could never say that. She had built her pride up again, inch by painful inch, here at Barton. She couldn't let it crumble away again.

'I couldn't give you an heir,' she said quietly. 'I couldn't be the kind of grand countess you needed. So I gave you the chance to move forwards in your own way.'

'Or perhaps you want the chance to marry that man Marton.'

Jane gave a choked laugh. Maybe she *had* harboured vague hopes of moving forwards with David Marton, or someone like him. Someone kind and peaceful, who wouldn't break her heart all over again. But that had only been a dream, so far from reality. She had to be done with dreams. They had never brought anything good.

'Sir David has been kind to me, yes,' she said as she turned away from Hayden and fussed with the clean bandages and the basin. 'So has his sister.'

'You've made many friends here, have you? To replace the ones you left in London?'

Jane didn't like his tone, dark and suspicious, almost disgruntled even. He had no right to be suspicious of *her*, not after all that had happened in London. Not after Lady Marlbury. She twisted the bandage in her fist.

'What friends did I ever have in London?' she said. 'Everyone we ever saw was *your* friend. I had to fit into your life, even if I was a very square peg in a very round hole. So, yes, I have made some friends here. The neighbours and the villagers are kind to Emma and me, they don't gossip about us. They don't laugh at us behind our backs. I'm not lonely here.'

'You were lonely in London?' he said and sounded incredulous. 'What did you not have there? What did I not give you? I tried to make you happy, Jane. I gave you what any woman could want.'

'Oh, yes,' Jane cried. She could feel her emotions, so tightly tied down for so long, springing free and spiralling beyond her control. The pain and anger she'd thought gone were still there. But so was the tenderness. 'You gave me houses, carriages, gowns and jewels. What else could a woman possibly want?'

Except love. A family. What she had wanted most when they married. There they had failed each other.

'What did you want from me, Jane?' he said, a near-shout.

'You left me alone.' She spun around to face him. Her handsome husband. The man she'd loved so much. *He* was all she had wanted. And he couldn't give her that. 'When the babies were—gone. When I tried to tell you what I needed. I was so alone, Hayden.'

He shook his head. There was such confusion in his eyes, even though she'd told him this before. Tried so hard to make him see. 'You just laid there in your room, Jane. You wouldn't go anywhere, wouldn't talk to anyone.'

'There was no one to talk to,' she whispered. Oh, she was so tired of this, of the pain that wouldn't end. It *had* to end. She had to end it.

She went and knelt down next to him with the bandages and quietly set about changing the dressings on his leg. It was hard to be so near him, to feel his heat, smell the familiar scent of him and know what couldn't be again. What had never really been, except in her imagination.

'Are you happy here, Jane?' Hayden asked softly.

She nodded, not looking up from her task. 'Barton is my home. I've found a—a sort of peace here.'

'And friends?'

'Yes. And friends. Emma and I belong here.'

He was silent for a long moment and sat very still under her nursing attentions. 'We cannot divorce. Surely you must know that.'

She nodded. She *had* always known that, even with that wild hope that made her write to him in the first place. Men like Hayden, with titles and ancient family names, couldn't divorce. Even when their wives proved unsatisfactory.

'But perhaps we can reach some arrangement that would work for both of us,' he said. 'I don't want to go on making you unhappy, Jane. I never wanted that.'

Surprised by the heaviness in his words that matched her own emotions, Jane glanced up at him. For just an instant there was a sad shadow in his eyes. Then he smiled and it was gone.

'My money should be good for something when it comes to you, Jane,' he said, lightly.

Jane grimly went back to her task. 'I never wanted your money.'

'I know,' he answered. 'But right now that's all I have to give you, it seems.'

* * *

Hayden frowned as he studied the array of silver items laid out before him on the cloth-covered dining-room table. Patches of each piece sparkled, but other patches were still dull and pock-marked, streaked in strange patterns.

'Blast it all,' he cursed as he threw down the polishing rag. He had to be very careful what he asked for here, it seemed.

When he hobbled downstairs at what he thought was a reasonably early hour for the country, Hannah the maid sniffily informed him that Lady Ramsay and Miss Emma were already working in the garden and, if he wanted breakfast, tea and toast would have to suffice. And when he had asked—nay, near begged for a task, she gave him this. Polishing the Bancroft silver that, from the looks of it, had been packed away for approximately a hundred years with no polish coming near it.

How hard could it be to polish a bit of silver while his leg healed up? Wipe things up a bit, maybe get Jane to smile at him again as she once did.

Not so easy as all that, it turned out. He polished and polished, only to partially clean up a smallish tray, a chocolate pot and a few spoons. The newly shining bits only seemed to make the rest of it look shoddier and there were still several pieces he hadn't touched at all.

Hayden had to laugh at himself as he tossed down the rag. It seemed 'butler' wouldn't be his new job. He would have to find some other way to surprise Jane.

Jane. Hayden ran his hands through his hair, remembering how she looked at him as she nursed his leg. For just the merest second there, he had dared to imagine that she even looked happy to see him again. For just a moment, it felt like it had when they were first together, and the laughter and smiles were easy.

And for just that second the hopes he had pressed down and locked away so tightly now struggled to be free again. He had to shove them away and forget them all over again. He had to just remember what came after those hopes died and he realised he could never

make Jane happy. That they were only an illusion to each other after all.

But there, in the quiet intimacy of the candlelight and the rain, with Jane's scent and
warmth wrapped around him again, it didn't
feel like an illusion. It felt more real, more
vital than anything else in his life.

Then those shadows drifted across her
eyes again and she turned away from him.
He still didn't know how to make her happy.

He pushed away the silver in front of
him and used his borrowed walking stick
to push himself to his feet. Labouring away
here all alone in this gloomy room wouldn't
make Jane smile at him again. And gloomy
it certainly was. It was a long, narrow, high-
ceilinged room, probably once very grand.
Now the furniture was shrouded in canvas,
and paler patches on the faded blue wallpaper showed where paintings had once hung.
The rug was rolled up and shoved against
the wall. Several crystals were missing from
the chandelier.

And yet Jane seemed happier here than
amid the fashionable grandeur of their London house.

Hayden heard a burst of laughter from beyond the closed dining-room doors. He limped over and eased it open to peer into the hall just beyond.

Jane and Emma had just come dashing in, apparently after getting caught in a sudden morning rain. Their hair tumbled down in damp ropes and Emma was shaking out a wet shawl.

Jane dropped the bucket she was carrying and shook out her wet skirts. The thin muslin clung to her body, which was as slender and delicate as ever, and just as alluring to him. But what caught his avid attention was the look on her face. She looked so alive, so happy and free as she laughed. Her eyes sparkled.

He remembered how it had felt that first time he took her hand, as if her warmth and innocence could be his. As if the life he had always led, the only life he knew, wasn't the only way he had to be. That he could find another path—with her.

Maybe it was this place, this strange, ramshackle, warm-hearted place, that had given his wife that air of laughing, welcoming life.

Because here she bloomed. With him she had faded and he had faded with her. Yet here she was, his Jane again.

His hope. And he had never, ever wanted to hope again.

'Well, Lady Ramsay. What do you think of your new home?'

Jane laughed as Hayden lifted her high in his arms and carried her over the threshold of Ramsay House. He twirled her around so fast she could see only blurry glimpses of an ancient carved ceiling and dark-panelled walls hung with bright flags and standards. It didn't look like an especially auspicious honeymoon spot, but Jane was so happy with Hayden she didn't care where she was.

From the outside, as they drove up in their carriage pulled by cheering estate workers, Ramsay House was a forbidding grey-stone castle, austere and sharp-lined. She half-expected knights to appear on the crenellated ramparts to throw boiling oil at her, but instead the steps were lined with smiling servants who tossed petals as she emerged from

*the carriage and called out, 'Best wishes to
Lord and Lady Ramsay!'*

Lady Ramsay. *The name still sounded so
strange. It couldn't possibly belong to her,
be her. The same hazy strangeness that had
enveloped her ever since she had walked up
the aisle to take Hayden's hand only vanished
when she was in his arms. There she felt as
if she belonged. There she never wanted to
be anyplace else.*

*'I'm sure it's lovely,' she said, laughing as
he spun her around faster and faster. 'But I
can hardly see it, Hayden!'*

*He finally twirled to a stop and slowly low-
ered her to her feet. They held on tightly to
each other as the room lurched to a stop
around them.*

*'You can make any changes you want to
it, of course,' Hayden said. 'You are the mistress of Ramsay House now.'*

*Jane tilted back her head to examine the
room closer. Just like the turrets and arrow
slits outside, the inside looked like nothing
so much as a medieval great hall. There
were even a few suits of slightly tarnished
armour, and ancient battleaxes and swords*

hung between the battle flags. There were no softening rugs or chintz cushions, no flower arrangements or haphazard piles of books, as she was used to at Barton Park.

'I don't think this place has had any changes made since about 1350,' she said uncertainly. And surely she wasn't going to be the one bold enough to tear it down and start again.

Hayden laughed. 'I don't think it has. About time for it to be brought into the nineteenth century, don't you think?'

Jane caught a glimpse of a painting hung at the far end of the room and hurried over to look at it more closely. Unlike the rest of the furnishings, it had a modern look about it. It was a family group, three people seated in a semi-circle in this very medieval space. An older man with his grey hair tied back in an old-fashioned queue, scowling above his tightly tied cravat, and a younger woman next to him, dressed in an elegant blue-silk gown and lace shawl. Her glossy black hair, piled high atop her head, matched that of the little boy playing with a toy sword at her feet.

It should have been a cosy family scene,

but the artist had captured some rather disquieting details. None of the three looked at each other. The woman had a distant, dreamy look in her eyes, where the man seemed unhappy at everything around him. The boy was also engrossed only in his toys. It almost seemed to be three separate paintings.

Jane felt Hayden come to stand behind her, his body warm against hers. 'This is you and your parents?' she said.

'Yes. I remember sitting for this—it was terribly dull and I was far too fidgety for my father's liking,' Hayden said, his tone deliberately light. 'This is the first thing you should get rid of. Banish it to the attics.'

Jane suddenly realised how very little she knew about Hayden's family. Only that he was an only child whose parents were long dead, much like her own. But nothing about what they were like when they were alive. 'What should we put in its place?'

'A portrait of you, of course. Or maybe not.'

'No?' Because she wasn't the real *Lady Ramsay?*

'*Maybe I would want to keep your image all to myself in my own chamber,*' he said teasingly.

Jane spun around and threw her arms around Hayden, unable to bear looking at the strangely melancholy painting any longer. She closed her eyes and breathed in deeply of his delicious, comforting scent.

'*Perhaps you should show me your chamber now,*' she said. '*So I can see what sort of painting might be needed.*'

Hayden laughed and scooped her up in his arms again. '*That is one command I can happily obey.*'

He carried her up the stone staircase and along what seemed to be endless twisting corridors, until he opened a door at the very end of the last hallway. Jane barely had a glimpse of a very large carved bed, a massive fireplace and green-velvet curtains at the windows before Hayden spun her around in his arms.

'*Blast it all, Jane, but I've been wanting to kiss you for hours and hours,*' he said hoarsely. '*All the way from London.*'

'*What are you waiting for, then?*' Jane

whispered. 'I've been wanting the very same thing...'

Their mouths touched softly at first, tasting, learning. Remembering last night after their wedding.

He kissed her so gently, once, twice, before the tip of his tongue traced her lower lip and made her gasp with the sudden rush of longing. She grabbed on to his shoulders tightly to keep from falling and whispered his name.

'My beautiful wife,' Hayden moaned, and pulled her even closer as their kiss caught fire. Their lips met in a burning clash of need and want, and the rest of the world completely vanished. There was only the two of them, bound together by a passion that refused to be denied.

And Jane knew that truly this was where she was meant to be. With Hayden. In his arms, there was no doubt, no fear. No worry that they were too young, that they had married too quickly. She had been right to say yes to Hayden.

They belonged together and that was all that mattered.

Chapter Six

Jane tossed the handful of weeds into a bucket and stood up to stretch her aching back. It was much like every other day here at Barton, taking advantage of the lull in the rain to work in the garden. Emma was darting around with a book in one hand and a trowel in the other, no doubt collecting more botanical specimens, while Murray chased sticks and barked, and their maid, Hannah, hung out the laundry.

And yet it wasn't like any other day, not really. Because Hayden sat on the terrace, watching them all.

Jane tried to ignore him. The clouds were gathering again and she had work to do in the garden before they were forced to go inside. In fact, she had been trying to ignore him completely for the two days he had been at Barton.

It hadn't been too hard to avoid him. He stayed in the guest chamber they had hastily cleared out. Hannah carried his meals to him, scurrying in and out as fast as she could. Emma took him books to read and Jane checked on the bandages after dinner. After their quarrel that first night, they were scrupulously polite, exchanging few words.

It made Jane want to scream. Careful, quiet, distant politeness had never been Hayden. That was what had drawn her to him in the first place, that vivid, bright life that burned in him like a torch. He shook up her careful life, turned it all topsy-turvy until she wanted to run and dance and shout along with him. Be alive with him.

She hadn't realised at the beginning the other side of that beckoning flame. She hadn't realised how very hard married life would be. She had been so young, so romantic, with so little experience of men like Hayden and their world. When she had left

London, she had wanted only the quiet she found at Barton, and that was her healing refuge. Her chance to get to know herself.

But quiet sat uneasily on Hayden. The silent tension between them, under the same roof, but not in the same world, only reminded her how long they had been apart.

She held up her hand to shade her eyes from the grey light and studied him as he sat on the terrace. His black hair shimmered, brushed back from the lean angles of his face, and his finely tailored green coat and elegantly tied cravat made him stand out from the shabbiness around him. His polished boot rested against the old chipped planter and he leaned on the walking stick Emma had unearthed from somewhere as he solemnly studied the garden.

He looked like a god suddenly dropped down from the sky. He didn't belong there any more than she belonged in London. They didn't belong *together*.

Yet he had dismissed any talk of divorce.

Jane sighed as she tugged off her dirty garden gloves. Soon enough he would be on his way, as soon as the doctor said he could travel. Then they could go back to their silent, distant truce, their limbo.

But she was afraid she would have to work at forgetting him all over again.

She made her way to the terrace and sat down on the old stone bench next to him. They were silent together for a moment, watching as Emma and her dog disappeared into the tangled entrance of the old maze.

'How are you feeling today?' Jane asked.

'Much better,' he answered. He gestured towards the maze with his stick. 'Should she be going in there?'

Jane laughed. 'Probably not. The maze hasn't been maintained in years, it's surely completely overgrown with who knows what. But it's hard to tell Emma what not to do. She is sure to do it, anyway.'

Hayden smiled down at her, the corners of his eyes crinkling in the light. 'Unlike her sister, I dare say,' he said teasingly.

'Very true. I always tried to do what I should.' Jane sighed to think of how hard she had worked to be what everyone wanted, to take care of everyone. And look how that ended up. 'I think Emma has the right idea.'

'I should have taken better care of you, Jane,' he said quietly.

Jane was shocked by those words. She turned to look at him, only to find that he still watched the garden. 'In what way? You said it yourself—you gave me everything I could want.'

'I gave you what I thought you must want. A fine house, a title, jewels, gowns.' He softly tapped the end of the stick on the old stones of the terrace, the only sign of movement about him. 'Yet it occurs to me that I never asked if *you* wanted them.'

'I— Yes, of course I did,' Jane said, confused. 'Emma and I never had a home after our parents died. It was all I wanted.' And, yes, she had wanted the title, too. It seemed to stand for continuity, security. Yet it turned into something very different indeed.

'But you didn't want *my* house. Not in the end.' Hayden suddenly turned to look at her, his bright blue eyes piercing. 'Are you happy here, Jane?'

'Very happy,' she said. 'Barton isn't a large place, as you've seen, and it needs a great deal of work. But it's my home. It reminds me of my parents, and when we were a family. It gives me a place to—to…'

'A place to belong,' Hayden said quietly.

Jane looked at him in surprise. She wasn't quite used to this Hayden, the man who listened to her, thought about what she really wanted and not what he thought she *should* want. 'Yes. I belong here. And I want Emma to feel that way, too.'

Once she'd wanted to give Hayden that as well. Wanted their home to be with each other. But that couldn't be in the end and there was no use crying any longer.

'Yes,' she said. 'A place to belong. Barton gives us that now. Leaky roof and everything.'

'Jane!' she heard Emma call, and she looked up to find her sister waving at her from the rickety old gate that guarded the entrance to the garden maze. Emma's hair was tangled, with leaves caught in the blonde curls, and her dress was streaked with dirt. 'Jane, I reached the maze's centre at last. Come see what I found.'

Jane laughed and hurried down the terrace steps towards her sister. She hadn't known what to say to Hayden. It was so long since he talked to her like that, since he looked at her as if he was trying to read her thoughts. It reminded her too much of the old Hayden, the one she knew all too briefly before he vanished.

She couldn't bear it if that Hayden reappeared now, when she had finally begun to get over him.

'Emma, whatever are you doing in there?' Jane said, laughing as Emma grabbed her hand. 'You look like a scarecrow.'

'Oh, never mind that,' Emma cried. 'You have to come see, Jane! It's the loveliest thing.' She glanced over Jane's shoulder and her delighted smile widened. 'You come, too, Ramsay. I must say, you are looking much more hale and hearty this morning.'

Jane turned to see that Hayden had left his seat on the terrace and was walking towards them on the overgrown pathway. The pale light gleamed on his hair and his smile seemed strangely unsure. Not his usual confident, carefree grin. It made her heart start to thaw just the tiniest bit more, made her want to run to him and take his hand.

He already seemed different here than she remembered when they parted. Quieter, more watchful, more careful. It utterly confused her.

But she knew one thing for certain. She could *not* be drawn back to Hayden Fitzwalter. She couldn't be caught up in the bright, chaotic whirlwind of him again. Her heart couldn't stand it.

'I'm sure Hayden should be resting, Emma,' Jane said. 'We can't drag him all over the garden.'

'Not at all,' Hayden said. 'I don't think I could stand to rest for another second without going crazy.'

Emma happily clapped her hands before grabbing Jane's arm and leading her through the entrance to the maze. Hayden followed them. Jane couldn't see him, but she could hear the tap of his stick on the gravel and feel the warmth of him just behind her.

The tangled hedge walls loomed around them, blocking out the day, and it seemed as if the three of them were closed into their own little world. Emma's dog barked somewhere ahead of them and the sound was muffled and echoing.

'How long has this maze been here?' Hayden asked.

'Oh, ages and ages,' Emma said. 'Since the Restoration at least. They were very fond of places where they could hide and be naughty, weren't they? But it hasn't been used in a long time.'

'When we were children, we were forbidden to come in here,' Jane said. 'My mother was sure we would be lost for ever and our nanny told us wild fairies lived in the hedges, just waiting to snatch up wayward children.'

'I never saw any fairies, though,' Emma said, sounding rather disappointed.

'But you come in here now?' said Hayden.

'Emma has begun exploring a bit,' Jane answered. 'I have enough work to do just tending the main flowerbeds.'

'It's too bad, because this could be so lovely,' Emma said. She tossed a quick grin back at them. 'Rather romantic, don't you think? Just imagine it—moonlight overhead, a warm breeze, an orchestra playing a waltz…'

'No more novel reading for you, Emma,' Jane said with a laugh. 'You are becoming too fanciful.'

Emma turned another corner, leading them further and further inwards. Jane saw now that her sister must have spent even more time exploring the maze than she had thought, for Emma seemed to know just where she was going.

'Not at all,' Emma said. 'But just picture it, Jane! Wouldn't this be a marvellous place for a costume ball? Especially *here.*'

They turned one more tangled corner and were in the very centre of the maze. Jane almost gasped at the sight that greeted them, it was so unexpected and, yes, so romantic.

Amid the octagonal walls was a small, open-sided summerhouse topped with a lacy cupola. It had once been painted white, but was now peeling to reveal the wooden planks beneath, and some of the boards had fallen away to land on the ground, but it was still a whimsical and inviting spot. An empty, cracked reflecting pool surrounded it, lined with statues of classical goddesses and cupids staring down at its lost glories.

Emma was right—this would be a perfect spot for a costume ball. With torches, music, dancing, the light on the pool…

And Hayden taking her in his arms to waltz her across the grass. She remembered he was such a good dancer, so strong and graceful that she had seemed to float at his touch. Had seemed to forget everything else but that they were together, holding each other, laughing with the exhilaration of the dance and being young and in love.

No! Jane shook her head, refusing to remember how it was to dance with Hayden. She hurried up the steps of the summerhouse, but if she was trying to escape that way she saw at once it wouldn't work. The round space was surrounded by wide benches that once held lush cushions and at its centre hung a swing.

Just like the one in the garden at Ramsay House.

Jane whirled around to leave, only to find that Hayden stood behind her on the steps. The overhanging roof cast him in a lacy pattern of shadows, half-hiding his face. He glanced around the small space, and she saw that he remembered, too.

'Push me higher, Hayden!'

He laughed in her memory, the sound as strong and clear and perfect as if that day had returned to the present. She felt again the heat of the sun on her skin, the way her loose hair tickled the back of her neck. His hands at her waist, holding her safe in the very same moment he sent her soaring.

'You can't go any higher, Jane,' he insisted. And yet she knew she could, only with him. She seemed to soar into the sky, so very free. Until she landed back on earth and Hayden kissed her, his lips so warm on hers, the passion between them flaming higher than the sun.

So very perfect.

But perfection never, ever lasted more than a moment.

Jane stared up at Hayden now, caught halfway between that golden day and the present hour. 'I—I don't think this swing would be safe to use.'

'Not like the one at the lake at Ramsay House,' he said quietly, roughly.

'Not at all like that one.' Jane brushed past him and hurried back down the steps. Emma was chasing Murray around the clearing, laughing, and Jane watched them as she tried to breathe deeply and remind herself that the Hayden she knew that day of the swing wasn't the real Hayden.

Just as that girl hadn't been the real Jane. That was all just a silly dream. Then she had lost the babies and she woke up.

She had to stay awake now, and guard her heart very, very carefully.

Had Jane always been so beautiful?

Hayden watched his wife as she ran along the garden pathway towards the terrace, laughing with her sister. Of course Jane had always been beautiful. She had drawn him in from the first moment he saw her, with the way all her emotions flashed through her large hazel eyes, with the shining loops of her dark hair he wanted to get lost in. Yes— Jane had always been so very beautiful.

But she had also been pale and somehow fragile, moving through the world so carefully. Everyone in London had wanted to emulate her, her elegant clothes and hats, everyone had wanted invitations to her small soirées. Yet still that air of uncertainty clung about her. He had been so sure he could banish it, that he could make her happy while still not making himself vulnerable. When he couldn't, the frustration and anger consumed him.

Here at Barton, Jane wasn't uncertain at all. Her pale skin had turned an unfashionable, but attractive, burnished gold. She was still slender, but she didn't look as if she would break. As she twirled around in a circle with her sister, laughing with glorious abandon, she looked carefree.

Happy.

That was what he wanted so much to give her, where he had failed. When they were together, he had watched that fragile hope in her eyes fade to silent sadness, but he couldn't seem to stop it, no matter how hard he tried. He couldn't really know what she wanted and he didn't have it in him to discover it. He didn't know how to even begin.

How could he? He had learned nothing of emotions and connections from his own parents, nothing but how to be what they and society expected him to be—a rake and a scoundrel. A failure. He didn't know how to be anything else, even for Jane.

For an instant, Jane and Emma's laughter faded and the overgrown gardens melted, and he stood before his father's massive library desk.

'Never was a man cursed with such a worthless heir!' the earl had roared, while Hayden's mother lounged on the sofa, drinking her ever-present claret and smirking at her son's latest peccadillo. It was all she ever did. *'If only your older brother had lived. You have disgraced us for the last time, Hayden. Obviously there is something in you, some curse from your mother's family, that won't allow you to be a true Fitzwalter. You are a wastrel and a fool, and I wash my hands of you! You are no son of mine.'*

It was during a diatribe very like that one that his father had an apoplexy and keeled over dead on the library carpet, not long after his mother died trying to give her husband one more son. So his 'wastrel' son killed him in the end. And Hayden never saw any reason to rise above the low expectations set for him so long ago.

Until Jane. By then it was too late. And he hadn't protected her from the very things that brought down his own parents. He couldn't fail her like that again.

'Hayden, come dance with us!' Emma called, twirling in a circle.

Hayden was jerked out of the sticky tentacles of the past and dropped back into the present moment in the garden at Barton. Emma ran over to grab his hand, and Jane watched him with a bemused half-smile on her face.

At least she wasn't frowning at him for the moment. He wished she would *really* smile at him again, as she had that day on the swing at Ramsay House. She had laughed then, too, letting her wariness drop away and letting herself be free with him. The memory of that smile was like a secret jewel he had cherished over all these years.

But he knew he hadn't yet earned another. Maybe he never would.

'I don't think Hayden is up to dancing yet, Emma,' Jane said. 'Besides, it looks like the rain is coming back. We should return to the house, don't you think?'

Emma pouted a bit, but nodded and dashed off after her dog towards the terrace. Jane picked up her bucket and looped it over her arm before she fell into step with Hayden as they made their slower way back.

'I hope we didn't keep you up too long today,' she said quietly. 'How does your leg feel?'

'Much better,' he answered. 'The exercise does me good. I could become far too indolent, lolling by your fire and eating your cook's cream cakes.'

Jane laughed. 'Somehow I can't picture you being indolent, Hayden. You were always dashing off to a race or a boxing match. Always seeking—something.'

'I don't feel like dashing around so much here,' Hayden said, and he was surprised to realise those words were true. In the few days he had been at Barton he found his whirling thoughts had slowed. He hadn't felt that old, familiar itch to be always going, doing. And not just because of his leg. Because of being around Jane again, around her serene smile.

He glanced down at Jane where she walked beside him. He knew now what it was he saw in her here, what he could never give her—contentment.

He looked back at the house. In the daylight it was easy to see how shabby Barton was, how many things needed to be done. New windows, the roof patched, the garden cleared. He remembered how Jane would speak of it after they were married, as if it was a tiny spot of paradise. A place of happy memories, so unlike his own family home. She'd wanted to visit it with him, but there was never time. Now he saw her 'paradise' was merely a small, ramshackle manor house. But she did seem happy there.

'You work too hard here, Jane,' he said.

She shrugged. 'I don't mind the work. I want to help Barton and working helps me forget—things.'

Things like the fact that she was married to him? Hayden stabbed his walking stick hard against the ground to try to ease the pang that thought gave him. 'You are just one person. These gardens are too much for you.'

'I can't do all I would like, of course,'

Jane said calmly, as if she was completely unaware of his inner turmoil. 'But real gardeners are expensive, so I do what I can.'

She was a countess, *his* countess. She shouldn't be working at all, Hayden thought fiercely. She should be lounging on a satin *chaise*, approving the designs of the best gardeners there were to be had and then watching her dreams take shape.

'I can tell you love it here,' Hayden said.

Jane really did smile then, a *real* smile that brought out the hidden dimple in her cheek he had once loved discovering. It almost felt as if the sun burst forth after a long, long night.

'I do love it,' she said. 'It's as if I can still sense my parents here and Emma is so happy. I know we can't go on like this for ever, but— yes, I love it here. I wish...' Her voice faded and she looked away from him.

'You wish what, Jane?' Hayden reached out to gently touch her hand and, to his surprise, she didn't pull away from him.

'I wish that we could have come here when we first met,' she whispered. 'That you could have seen it then.'

'Do you think things would have been different?'

Jane shrugged again. 'I don't know. Perhaps not. We are really such different people inside. I was just too foolish to see it then. Or maybe I just didn't want to see it. But at least we could have been together here for a while.'

They reached the terrace and Jane turned away to put down her bucket. 'Do you feel like dining with us tonight?' she said. 'It won't be London cuisine, but one of the neighbours did send over some venison today and cook makes a fine stew.'

One of the neighbours—like that David Marton? Hayden remembered how she had smiled at the man, how he seemed to belong here in a way Hayden himself never really could.

'I'd be happy to dine with you tonight,' Hayden said tightly. 'I'm feeling much better, Jane, really. I should be out of your way very soon.'

Jane glanced at him, an unreadable gleam in her eyes. 'There's no hurry, Hayden. Not when you are just beginning to recover here.'

She slipped through the doors into the house, leaving Hayden alone on the terrace. He studied the overgrown gardens, the tangled flowerbeds and the ragged pathways. He *had* failed Jane. He had not been able to make her happy. But he saw now there was one thing he could give her that would surely make her smile.

If he could just find a way to make her accept it.

'Did you have a dog when you were young, Hayden?' Emma asked. 'Do you remember it?'

Hayden grinned at her. He couldn't *help* but smile at her as she gambolled with her puppy in front of the fire after a most congenial dinner. There had been much laughter and chatter about inconsequential, funny things. Even Jane had laughed and exchanged a warm glance or two with him across the small table.

Or at least he fancied she did. Hoped she did.

Jane definitely smiled now as she looked up from the account book she studied.

'Hayden is not exactly old and decrepit now, Emma. I'm sure he can remember whether or not he had a dog.'

'Despite my stick? And my grey hairs?' Hayden said, waving the stick in the air. He nearly had no use for it any longer, yet he found himself strangely loath to let it go. It would mean he was well enough to leave Barton Park and he wasn't ready to do that.

Emma made a face, and tossed a ball across the room for Murray to run after. 'Of course you aren't old, Hayden. Just—oldish.'

'Thank you very much for the distinction,' Hayden choked out, trying not to fall over laughing.

'So,' Emma went on, 'did you have a dog?'

'Not a good dog like Murray,' he said. 'My father was quite the country sportsman and kept a pack of hounds, but I wasn't supposed to go near them. And my mother had a rather vicious little lapdog who loathed everyone but her. But she quite adored it for some strange reason.'

Emma's pretty face crumpled. 'Oh, poor Hayden! Everyone should have a dog to love.

You must play with Murray whenever you like.'

As if Murray agreed, he bounded up to Hayden and dropped his slimy toy ball at Hayden's feet, marring his polished shoes.

'Er—thank you very much,' Hayden muttered doubtfully.

'I'm not sure Hayden would really thank you for the favour,' Jane said. 'Emma, dear, could you fetch me the green ledger book from my desk in the library? I need to check something here.'

Emma nodded, still looking most saddened by Hayden's lack of boyhood pets, and hurried out at a run with Murray at her heels. Hayden glanced over at Jane and found her regarding him with something in her eyes he hadn't seen in a very long time—sympathy.

It made him want to snatch her up in his arms and hold her so very close, twirl her around in sudden bursts of joy as he once did when he would come home to Ramsay House and find her waiting for him so eagerly. Yet hard-learned caution kept him in his seat, across the room from her. He didn't want to frighten her, not with everything hanging between them so delicate and tentative.

'Emma is most enthusiastic in her interests,' he said.

Jane laughed. 'Indeed she is. And you are very kind to her. I suppose it's a good thing I never wanted a lapdog in London, they sound like fearsome little beasties.'

'Oh, they most certainly are. Fifi was fierce in guarding my mother and biting everyone else who ventured near, a veritable tiny Cerberus. But if you *had* wanted one, if it would have made you smile, I would have fetched one in a trice and laid it at your feet.'

Her smile flickered and she looked down at the book open in front of her. 'A dog might have added a little—warmth to the house, I suppose. But not one that would insist on biting the ankles of every caller. I wouldn't want to drive away all my friends.'

Hayden couldn't stop himself asking—he had to know. 'It wasn't all so very bad, was it, Jane? We had some good times.'

She glanced up at him, and her hazel eyes were bright. A tentative smile touched her lips. 'No, it certainly wasn't all bad. I remember some lovely moments indeed.'

'Like when the estate workers at Ramsay House unhitched our carriage horses and pulled us to the house themselves for the honeymoon?'

Her smile widened, giving him a quick glimpse of the sweet, wondrous girl he'd first met. A quick moment to dare to hope. 'And when I found you had ordered my chamber filled with flowers! I could barely move in there.'

'And when we swam in the lake?'

'You were a terrible swimmer,' she said, really laughing now. 'I thought you had drowned for one terrible moment.'

'I only did that so you would feel sorry for me and kiss me.'

'Which I did—and more, much more there in the summerhouse.' Her cheeks suddenly turned pink, and she turned away. 'No, it wasn't all bad. I was just so young then, so foolish. I thought everything would always be just that way.'

'We aren't so young now, Jane. We've been married five years and spent barely two of those years together,' Hayden said, suddenly feeling very urgent. Somehow they had to connect again. 'Surely we can talk. Perhaps I could even make you see me as you once did. The real me.'

For she was the only one who had ever *truly* seen him, just him, Hayden the man and not the earl. The man he was and the man he really wanted to be. And like an idiot he had thrown that rare treasure away.

Emma came running back in just at that moment, not giving Jane time to answer. But she *did* smile at him and, for the moment, that would have to be enough. Until he put his plan in order.

'Keep your eyes closed,' Hayden said sternly as he helped his wife down from the carriage.

Jane laughed and shook her head, but she didn't move away from his guiding hands on her shoulders or try to remove the blindfold tied over her eyes. 'This is ridiculous, Hayden! I have seen your town house before.'

'It wasn't my town house,' he said. 'It was my parents'. More accurately, my mother's

since my father did not care for it. But now it is our *town house. I've had it completely refurbished, attics to kitchens, to make it ours.'*

He helped her up the marble steps just as Makepeace, the butler who had presided over this place ever since Hayden was in leading strings, opened the front door and gave a deep bow. 'Welcome home, my lord, my lady. I trust you had a pleasant time in the country.'

'Most refreshing, thank you, Makepeace,' Hayden said.

Jane stumbled a bit on the top step, but Hayden held her fast with his strong arms. Refreshing said the very least of it. It had been—amazing. Beautiful. Transcendent. She had never imagined being so close to another person could be so wonderful.

He led her through the grand rooms, the beautiful drawing room decorated in the very latest à la greque *fashion, the music room with its gilded pianoforte and harp, the dining room with its vast expanse of polished table and many, many perfectly aligned, brocade-cushioned chairs waiting for elegant parties.*

Parties she would have to host.

A full-length portrait of Hayden's beautiful black-haired mother, in full countess splendour in velvet robes and coronet, peered down at her haughtily from her carved frame. A little white dog peeked out from her fur-trimmed hem, but it didn't make her look at all cosy. She looked rather fearsome. And now her job was Jane's. Her world was Jane's and it was one Jane knew hardly anything about.

Suddenly some of her silvery glow of happiness tarnished at the edges.

But Hayden still held her hand, and she clung to it. He led her up the stairs and into a large suite of rooms, all done in blue-and-silver satin, with a massive carved bed curtained and draped in blue velvet and piled with embroidered cushions. A dressing gown, all frothed with swathes of tulle, was spread with a dazzling array of silver and crystal pots and bottles and brushes.

'And this is yours,' Hayden announced proudly. 'I had it completely redecorated for you in a way you would love. My room

is right there through that door, so we can be together every night.'

Together every night. *Jane wished the night would start right away as she stared around the overwhelmingly elegant room. A room fit for a countess. A room fit for a woman she was not. How could she make this room, this life, her own?*

She suddenly felt very, very cold. Ramsay House had been a dream and she was waking up.

She slowly untied the ribbons of her bonnet and looked about for somewhere to put it down. A maidservant she hadn't even seen bustled over to take it with a curtsy.

'Do you like it?' Hayden said confidently. He was already sure she had to. It was the best of everything after all.

But it was not the room she would choose. A comfortable, shabby, pretty pink room for reading and talking—and kissing. 'It is beautiful.'

'I'm very glad to hear it.' Hayden kissed her cheek quickly and strode towards the closed connecting door. 'Settle in, enjoy yourself. Ring for the servants if you need

anything at all. I'm going to change my clothes and go to the club just for a while. It's been some time since I've seen my friends.'

'The club!' Jane whispered. He was leaving her, right now, all alone in this new house.

'Just for a short time. You must be tired from the journey, you won't want me hanging about while you rest. Mary will bring you supper here on a tray, won't you, Mary?'

'Of course, my lord,' the maid said quickly. 'I am here to help her ladyship with anything at all.'

'There you go, my dear,' Hayden said with a smile. He was obviously happy to be back in town. With or without her. 'Look around the house, let me know if you want to change anything.'

And then he was gone, the door swinging closed between them. Jane slowly sat down on a chaise by the marble fireplace and shivered, wishing a fire was laid. But it wasn't the chilly house making her cold. It was the sudden realisation, as quick and unwelcome *as a dunking in a snowbank, that this was her life now, her life as a countess. And she had no idea how to begin it.*

Chapter Seven

'Lord Ramsay sent this to you, my lady,' Hannah announced, in a grand voice Jane had never heard from the maid before. 'Grand' was never required at Barton.

She looked up in surprise from the trunk she was sorting through with Emma. Hannah stood in the bedchamber doorway, holding out a neatly folded note on a silver tray she had unearthed from somewhere.

'Isn't Lord Ramsay downstairs, Hannah?' Jane asked, dusting off her hands on her apron.

'Yes, my lady. In the old library.'

'Then why would he...?' Jane stared at the note. Yesterday in the maze, and then later at dinner with Emma, had been—different. Laughing with Hayden, talking with him rather than quarrelling, she was sure she caught a glimpse of the man she once thought she had married. He seemed serious, interested in life at Barton. There was even a strange, swift flash of sadness she couldn't quite work out, lost quickly in the laughter of a game of Pope Joan with Emma.

But then today the rain started again and Hayden retreated to her father's dusty old library. Now he was sending her notes instead of coming to talk to her. She was completely baffled by him.

'Aren't you going to read it?' Emma asked.

Jane suddenly realised Emma and Hannah were staring at her, their eyes wide with curiosity. 'Yes, of course,' she said briskly and reached for the letter.

It wasn't sealed, and when she unfolded it she saw Hayden's familiar bold, untidy scrawl. She remembered the last time she saw that handwriting, on the notes he would secretly send her behind her aunt's back when they were courting. She still had them, carefully tied up in ribbon at the bottom of her jewel case, unread since those heady days.

Would you do me the honour of having supper with me in the dining room at seven this evening? Sincerely, Hayden.

Jane almost laughed aloud at the absurdly formal words.

'What is it, Jane?' Emma asked.

'He invites me to dine,' Jane answered, folding the note and tucking it in her apron pocket. 'In my own house?'

'Indeed?' Emma said. Her voice sounded far too innocent. Jane turned to study her sister's face, which was written with a comical expression of false surprise.

'What do you know about this?' Jane demanded.

'Why, nothing at all! It sounds as if he would just like to spend time with you,' Emma said. 'Maybe he's just not sure *you* want to spend time with *him*.'

Spend time with Hayden? Once that had been all Jane wanted in the world, but it had never come to pass. He was always rushing away somewhere.

But now he was here in her house, trapped

by the weather and his injury, and he wanted to dine with her. What would they even have to say to each other, after all this time?

Yet she had to admit—she was curious. And just the tiniest bit excited.

'Will you go?' Emma asked.

'Of course. I have to eat some time,' Jane said. She turned back to Hannah. 'You may tell his lordship I will meet him in the dining room at seven.'

Emma clapped her hands as Hannah left with the message. She whirled back to the trunk they had been sorting through and tossed out a pile of gowns. They spread over the faded carpet like a vivid rainbow of shimmering silks and delicate muslins.

'What will you wear?' Emma said. She caught up a pale blue silk trimmed with dark blue velvet ribbons and pearl beading. 'This one? It's very pretty and the colour would look splendid with your eyes.'

Jane knelt down to study the tangle of dresses. Much like Hayden, they seemed like visitors from another world, this rich array from the finest London modistes. She had brought out the trunk only a few weeks ago when Emma needed a dress for the assembly. Once upon a time, shopping for these gowns had been a consolation to her, a refuge of sorts. She hadn't wanted to see them, remember the places she once wore them. The grand parties where she hadn't been able to measure up to society beauties.

The blue gown had gone to a reception at Carlton House, where she had dined amid the most luxurious of furnishings and watched tiny fish swim down a channel along the middle of the dining table. Where there was music and champagne and buffet tables piled with delicacies, all for the most illustrious people in the land. But what she remembered from that night was watching Hayden laughing and whispering with the statuesque, red-headed Lady Marlbury.

A woman who was rumoured to have been Hayden's mistress before he married. And that night it looked very much as if they were renewing the connection.

Jane carefully laid aside the blue gown and took up a pink muslin trimmed with cherry satin and froths of cream-coloured lace. It had gone to a garden party, which she had attended alone with some so-called friends. Hayden wasn't even there.

'This one, I think,' Jane said.

'It's very pretty. You should let me dress your hair,' Emma said. 'We could use some of the red rosebuds from the garden to make a wreath.'

Her sister sounded far too enthusiastic about hair and gowns. 'Emma, did you have a hand in this strange dinner invitation?'

Emma started to shake her head, but then she nodded sheepishly. 'Not very much, though. When I showed Hayden the library this morning, he asked me to help him inspect the dining room, too. That's all. Really, Jane, I think he just wants to talk to you alone, in a civilised setting.'

'But why go to the trouble? He only needs to come up here and ask to talk to me.' Though Jane was sure they had said everything they needed to say to each other. Talking now would only rip open old wounds. Make her want things she knew were lost, just as she had when Hayden laughed with her last night.

Emma shrugged. 'I don't know. But I do

think he wants to try to fit in here. Just be nice to him, Jane, please.'

'I'm always nice!' Jane protested. And she had tried with Hayden. Tried until she couldn't bear to try again.

She slipped her hand into her apron pocket and felt the crackle of the note there. Maybe, just maybe, she could dig deep and find it in herself to try one more time? Just for dinner?

'Help me find the pink slippers that go with the gown, Emma,' she said. 'They should be in here somewhere...'

Emma hummed a little tune as she skipped down the stairs, Murray's claws skittering on the wooden floor behind her. From behind the closed dining-room door she could hear the sound of furniture being moved, the clink of fine porcelain and silver being unpacked, and upstairs Jane was dressing in some of her pretty London clothes.

It was more activity than Barton had seen in a very long time and it felt as if the house was waking up around them. As if a whole new day was dawning.

Emma turned towards the library and gave

a little spinning turn on the newly polished floor. Everything was going so very well. Jane looked happier, smiling more, even laughing, and no one deserved to be happy more than her sweet sister did. And Hayden wasn't the ogre Emma had come to imagine when she had seen how distant Jane was in their first weeks back at Barton last year.

Emma didn't know the whole tale of her sister's marriage. Jane had never been one to confide her troubles in anyone else, just as Emma never told Jane about Mr Milne. But Emma's imagination had filled in tales based on novels she read about city lives and gossip from the girls at her old school. Hayden became almost a monster of unkindness and rakedom in her mind.

But when she found him injured on the road and brought him home, she'd seen he wasn't what she imagined. He seemed almost like Jane. Sad—seeking.

Of course, that didn't mean Emma wouldn't kill him if he dared hurt Jane again.

She closed the library door behind her and hurried to the shelf where she spent so much time, the section that held volumes and documents on the history of Barton and the neighbourhood. That was where she had found the original journal and where she had come to think the maze held the secrets to the treasure. She had to keep on with the hunt; she was so close now.

Jane slowly made her way down the stairs, hugging her wool shawl closer around her shoulders. Somehow the house, *her* house, felt strange, as if she walked through halls and rooms she had never seen before. Lamps were lit along the way, the flickering amber light blending with the waning daylight streaming through the windows. It made everything look magical.

Jane pressed her hand against her stomach to still the nervous flutters. It was ridiculous to be anxious. She was merely going to have a meal in her own house, with Hayden.

Alone with Hayden. That was the uncertain point. For such a long time, when they were alone they either fought or fell into each other's arms. Neither had ever done them much good. She'd spent all those months at

Barton trying to forget and find a way to move forwards.

She'd even thought she *had* moved forwards, until he suddenly appeared on her doorstep. Until yesterday, when she saw that swing and remembered all the good things that once were. Until he laughed with her and Emma, as if the past was truly past.

She hurried through the drawing room, towards the closed double doors that led into the dining room. They seldom used those rooms any longer and the furniture was shrouded with canvas covers. It made everything feel even stranger, more unreal, as did the echoing quiet of the house. Usually Emma and her dog were running around, the cook was banging pots and pans as loudly as she could in the kitchen and Hannah was singing as she dusted.

For such a small household, they made a lot of noise. Far more than the fully-staffed, impeccably run London house. But tonight even Emma was being quiet.

Jane paused as she reached for the door handle. She couldn't hear anything in the dining room. What if Hayden wasn't really there? What if he had changed his mind and run off back to London, despite the muddy roads?

Half-sure she would find the room empty, she pushed open the door.

The long table, which had been covered and empty for so long, was polished to a high gleam, set off by dozens of candles lit along its length and set on the sideboard. Two places were set at the far end with her mother's china and silver that had been packed away for safekeeping, and wonderful, enticing scents of cinnamon and stewed fruit emanated from the covered dishes on the sideboard. Her mother's portrait had even been taken from the attic and hung back in its old place on the faded wallpaper.

Jane took it all in, amazed at the transformation, until her gaze landed on Hayden. He stood behind the chair at the head of the table, dressed in a fine velvet-trimmed blue coat and faultlessly tied cravat, his glossy black hair smoothed back from his face.

'Have I suddenly been transported to a different house?' she said with a laugh. 'This can't possibly be Barton Park.'

A smile cracked his cautious façade and he hurried over to take her hand. He raised it to his lips for a soft, lingering kiss, and Jane shivered at the sensation of his mouth on her skin. It had been so very long since she had felt that. She'd forgotten the immediate, visceral reaction she always had to his touch.

'It's amazing what a bit of polish can do,' Hayden said as he led her to the chairs. 'Emma found the china and most of the candle holders in the attic, along with the portrait.'

'I knew she was up to something!' Jane cried. 'She is becoming much too good at subterfuge.' She sat down in the chair Hayden held out and arranged her skirts as she watched him sit down next to her. The candlelight shimmered over him, turning his skin to purest pale gold.

'She seemed very excited to help me set up a small surprise for you,' Hayden said. He reached for a ewer of wine and filled their glasses. 'She agrees with me—you work far too hard here.'

Jane sipped at the sweet, rich red liquid

and wondered where he'd unearthed it. 'I told you, I like the work. It keeps me occupied.'

'And there was nothing to keep you occupied in London?'

Jane set the glass down with a thump. 'Did you bring me here to quarrel again, Hayden?'

He shook his head. 'The very last thing I want to do is quarrel with you, Jane. I'm so weary of that and you deserve better.'

'Do I?' She swallowed hard past a sudden lump in her throat. She did deserve better; they both deserved better than the half-life they had lived together. She'd always wanted him to see that, to tell him that things could be different, but she had never found the right words. Until she didn't believe it herself.

Hannah hurried in with a tureen of soup and Jane couldn't say anything at all. As they sampled the first courses of what looked like the most elaborate meal Barton had seen in a long time, she asked him about his friends in London, how Ramsay House was faring, anything but the two of them. Anything but what happened between them before.

Anything but the lost babies.

And slowly, as the candles sputtered lower

and the darkness gathered outside, as Hannah served the elaborate meal and more wine was poured, something very strange happened. Jane started to enjoy herself.

'Oh, that didn't really happen!' she said, laughing helplessly. 'I can't even believe it.'

'Of course it really happened.' Hayden grinned at her, looking rather like a naughty schoolboy telling a joke he knew he shouldn't. 'You remember Lady Worthington's pet monkey. She always insisted on taking the blasted thing to every party and it always escaped.'

'Yes, but her footmen also captured the poor creature before it could wreak too much havoc.'

'Not this time. The wretched thing proved too wily for everyone and stole Prinny's hairpiece before carrying it up to the chandeliers. When he dropped it into the soup, Mrs Carlyle swore it was an immense African spider and, in all her shrieking and flailing, tore the cloth right off the table. Along with all the dishes. Luckily the bottle of port right in front of me was spared.'

Jane pressed her napkin to her mouth,

giggling at the wild images Hayden's dry, matter-of-fact rendition of the tale conjured up in her mind. She had forgotten that about Hayden—that he could be so very much *fun*. That he could see the ridiculous in any event and make her see it, too.

'I do wish I had seen that,' she said. 'But I'm glad Emma didn't. She would have demanded a pet monkey.'

Hayden refilled her wine glass and she suddenly realised that his was still half-full. He had been drinking remarkably little that night.

'To keep the dog company?' he said. 'That creature barks more than any canine I've ever seen. Perhaps he needs a friend.'

'She does adore Murray,' Jane said, sipping at the wine. It felt good to sit and just talk with Hayden, to be comfortable with him. Even though she knew such a moment couldn't last long, not with them. 'He was the runt of a litter one of the local farmers had and she rescued him. He's better than the last pet. It was a hedgehog and a rather ill-tempered one.'

'She said she collects plant specimens as well.'

'Oh, yes. She'll show you her laboratory if you give her the slightest encouragement.'

Hayden sat back in his chair and watched her, a half-smile on his lips. 'You *are* happy here, aren't you, Jane?'

'Of course,' she answered in surprise. She'd thought Hayden was far beyond noticing or caring whether she was happy or unhappy. Surely he could never think someone could be happy in the country. 'It's always been my home. You would think it much too quiet, though. The most excitement we ever have is when the vicar comes to call, or there's an assembly in the village.'

'They say the hunting is good around here,' he said. He toyed with the stem of his glass between his long, elegant fingers, and Jane found herself mesmerised by the movement. By a flashing memory of what those beautiful hands could do.

She tore her stare away from him and took a quick bite of the lemon-trifle dessert on her plate. She nearly choked on it. 'It is. My grandparents even helped start the local hunt club—they were avid riders. I'm sure Emma would enjoy the sport, too, but we can't afford to keep horses.'

Hayden nodded and Jane noticed that a shadow seemed to flicker over his face. But he never stopped the slow, lazy turning of the glass. 'You could let me help you, Jane.'

'No,' she said, suddenly feeling cold. 'No, I can't do that.'

'As much as you seem to want to fight the fact, I *am* your husband,' he said, so calm, so rational. It almost made her want the old, heated quarrels they had when he drank. They were easier for her to dismiss than this new, quiet, solemn Hayden. The man who was a stranger and yet also someone she knew so intimately.

'As if I could ever forget that,' she said.

'Then let me help you. It's the least I can do after how I treated you.'

'How you treated me?' Jane choked out. Like when they fought? Like when she only wanted his attention, the one thing that wasn't hers? Like when he refused to understand her? Or when she refused to understand him. Refused to try to fit into his world, because it was not hers at all.

'I wasn't all I should have been,' he said. 'I didn't really know how to be a husband. We were so young when we married. But I would like to learn how to be your friend, if you will let me. The past is gone. We must live in the present.'

Before Jane could even think out what to say to those extraordinary words, Hannah hurried in to gather the plates from the table. Jane slumped back in her chair, glad of the interruption, the moment to gather her scattered thoughts. Hayden was right—going over old quarrels, things that were past and done, would do them no good. They had to find a way to move forwards. But how? How could she stop the pain, once and for all?

Especially when he sat right beside her, with his beautiful eyes, the warmth and smell of him, reminding her of all she had once hoped for. All she still might long for, deep down inside, if she couldn't keep those wild emotions tightly bound down.

'Walk with me on the terrace?' Hayden said as Hannah left the room, china clattering. 'I think the rain has stopped and it's a fine night outside.'

Jane nodded. She could use the fresh air, the chance to clear her head and speak to him rationally again. When he drew back her chair and offered her his arm, she hesitated for a moment before she took it. He felt so warm and strong under her touch, so familiar and yet so foreign all at the same time. Her head whirled with how quickly they could veer now between distant politeness and falling back to the old intimacy.

Hayden led her through the old glass doors on to the terrace, limping just the merest amount on his bad leg. He had left the walking stick behind tonight. The night was dark and cloudy, lit only by the diluted, chalky rays of moonlight and the candles in the windows. In the distance she saw the maze, dark and mysterious, almost frightening, but the only thing she was really, vividly aware of was Hayden at her side.

'Do you remember the night of the Milbanke ball?' Hayden asked quietly.

Jane laughed. 'Of course. How could I forget? That was when you first asked me to

marry you. I was shocked out of my wits.
You probably were, too.' They'd walked on
a terrace much like this one, hiding in the
shadows together while the noise and colour of the party whirled on beyond the open
doors.

'I *was* shocked,' Hayden said. 'I never
meant to blurt out those words to you like
that, with no skill or charm. But once I said
it—I knew it was right.'

Jane leaned on his arm and closed her eyes
as she thought back to that night. It seemed
so long ago now, those shimmering moments
when it seemed as if every impossible dream
was coming true. It also seemed so close
now, on this other warm, soft night.

Yet they weren't the same people they
were then. She had been so disappointed so
many times until that hope simply withered
away. Surely Hayden felt the same. It became
so clear to her that he thought he was getting
something, someone, else when he married
her. That they didn't really know each other
at all. They had met and married in such
quick, dizzying succession.

But that night at the Milbanke ball had

been pure magic. So perfect that even now she felt the memory of it wrap around her and enfold her completely in its beautiful illusion.

'I thought it was right, too,' she whispered. 'When you kissed me, it felt like perfection, and I was sure we could never be parted again. But life can't always be like that.'

Hayden suddenly stopped, and Jane opened her eyes to blink up at him. His face was concealed in the night and he turned to clasp both her hands in his. 'I wanted to make everything perfect for you, Jane,' he said roughly. 'I wanted to make you smile every day, to erase that worry in your eyes once and for all. Instead I only made your life more difficult.'

Jane was astonished at his words, so stark and simple, so laden with hurt. After they married, he had kept every vestige of true emotion, true thoughts, hidden from her behind the wild whirl of parties and the fashionable life. She never would have imagined he felt that way at all.

'I was the one who was wrong,' she said. 'I was so silly, so sheltered behind my eccentric family. I didn't know what being your wife, being a countess, really meant. I could only see *you*. I only wanted to be with you. But marriage is never just two people, is it? It's so much more.'

He was quiet for a long, tense moment, until Jane feared she'd said something wrong. She tried to slip her hands out of his, but he wouldn't let her go.

'When I was growing up, my parents didn't talk to me often. When they did it was always about duty,' Hayden said. 'The duty of a Fitzwalter, of an earl.

He laughed, but Jane could hear the bitter tinge to it. Hayden never spoke of his parents to her when they were together, or of his life before he met her. She knew nothing about them, except that they died years before, his father of an apoplexy and his mother in childbirth.

'Hayden...' she began, desperate to tell him that his attractions as a husband to her had been everything about him *but* his title. His humour, his sense of fun, his good looks, the way he held her hand, the way she felt when he kissed her—she had wanted all those things so much. The title scared her to tears. The life he led in London scared her in its strangeness.

And she had been right to fear it in the end.

'No, Jane, let me say this,' he said. 'I wanted to give you everything I could, everything I thought you wanted. But I could give you nothing, could I? Not even a child.'

Jane's stomach seized with a sharp pain at the mention of the babies. That one thing she'd longed for above all others—Hayden's child, a new family, a new start. The thing that would never be. She would be too afraid of the pain even to try now.

'Hayden, please, no' was all she could say. She closed her eyes against the tears she couldn't afford to cry any more and tugged at her hands. Still he held on to her.

'I'm sorry, Jane,' he said simply, starkly. 'I'm sorry.'

'Oh, Hayden,' she choked out. 'Once those words were all I wanted from you. But now...'

'Now it's too late,' he said, a terrible ring of finality in those four simple words.

They stood there together in silence, holding hands, so close she could hear his breath, yet far apart. As far as the moon behind the haze of clouds.

'Dance with me,' Hayden suddenly said.

'D-dance? What about your leg?' Jane stammered. As usual, Hayden was too quick-silver for her.

'Like we did at the Milbanke ball. And my leg is fine. Perfectly up to a simple waltz.'

'There's no music.'

'Just imagine it. Remember it.'

His arm slid around her waist and the fingers of his other hand twined with hers. He drew her much closer than he had that night, under the watch of her aunt. Their bodies were pressed so close together she could feel his heartbeat echo through her.

He hummed the tune of that remembered waltz under his breath, ragged and out of tune and far too endearing. He was still the marvellous dancer she'd once known, despite his leg, and soon they were spinning and twirling over the terrace, his arm guiding her steps until they once again moved as one. Faster and faster, until Jane laughed helplessly and clung to him.

They whirled to a stop, out of breath, hearts pounding. Jane stared up at him, marvelling that she could fall into him again so quickly.

'It's been so long since I danced,' she said.

'Jane,' he said hoarsely and she saw a light shift in his eyes. Suddenly his arm tightened around her and his mouth came down to touch hers.

She went up on tiptoe as he kissed her, twining her arms around his neck to hold him against her. She felt his touch at her waist, dragging her even closer.

They still fit together so perfectly, their mouths, their bodies, their touch, as if they were made to be just so. Her body still wanted his so very much, still remembered every night they'd had together. She parted her lips and felt the tip of his tongue touch hers and the kiss slid down into frantic need. She wanted this so much, wanted to forget the past and have only *now*. To fall into him and be lost all over again.

Her head fell back as his lips trailed away from hers and he pressed a hot kiss to the sensitive curve of her neck. She shivered as his mouth trailed over her shoulder, the soft upper swell of her breast above her bodice. He remembered every spot that made her most wild with want for him.

She buried her fingers in the silk of his hair and sighed at the intense feelings that poured through her. At the connection that still coursed between them like lightning.

She felt him draw back, felt his kiss slide away from her, but he still held her against him. His arms were around her waist, pulling her up so his chin could rest atop her head. The rough, uneven rhythm of their breath mingled. Their heartbeats pounded out a frantic drum tattoo of need and want and fear.

Jane caressed his shoulder, her hand shaking.

'Oh, Jane,' he muttered. 'You see what you still do to me?'

She laughed. 'This was always the easy part between us, Hayden. Kissing, lovemaking—it was always so perfect. So wonderful. It always made us forget everything else.'

But 'everything else' always waited there, lurking in the shadows around them. It always came back to remind her that Hayden didn't, couldn't, love her as she longed for.

'Jane…' he began, but she backed away from him, shaking her head. She didn't *want* all those other things, not now, not on a night that had been so special.

And she definitely did not want to cry in front of Hayden. 'I must go look in on Emma,' she managed to whisper. 'Thank you for dinner, Hayden, and for our dance. It was—delightful.'

And she spun around and ran away before he could see her tears.

Hayden watched Jane go, her skirts swirling around her as she hurried up the stairs. He wanted to follow her more than he had ever wanted anything in his life, but something even more powerful held him back. Something that told him if he pushed her now, if he grabbed her in his arms and refused to let her go, she would drift even further away from him.

He raked his fingers through his hair, listening as her rushing footsteps faded away and the door to her room closed. He sat down on the step and braced his fists on the old, warped wood as he tried to make sense of all that happened tonight.

Hayden did not like to think. Drinking, carousing, horse racing, dancing—they erased the need for thought, for doing anything but being in that one moment. It had been like that his whole life, just as it had been for his father before him. Nothing else mattered then, not being the earl, not what he had failed to do. Only the speed and movement, the slow slide into forgetfulness.

But Jane had made him stop and think from the first time he saw her. Her quiet seriousness made him see things in a different way, made him *want* to be better. That he failed at that wasn't her fault. He'd chased her away and run back into his old ways. Almost forgotten how he felt when he was with her.

Only a few days back in her company, and it all came rushing out again. Without the barrier of drinking between them, he saw how Jane was here in the country. The pale, brittle, fragile Jane he remembered from the last days in London was gone. She was beautiful and strong here. And deeply, deeply

wary of him. Rightfully so. He had failed her
as a husband. He hadn't even really tried.

Hayden pounded his fists hard against
the stairs as he envisioned the raw pain in
Jane's eyes when he mentioned the babies.
He hadn't been there for her then; she didn't
want him here now.

He had to find a way to change again.

'How did the dinner go?' he heard Emma
ask, breaking into his brooding thoughts.

He looked up to see her leaning over the
banister from the landing, staring down at
him. Her blonde hair tangled over her shoulders and she held a squirming Murray under
her arm. For once even the puppy was quiet.

He shook his head and Emma groaned.
'That bad, was it?' she said as she hurried
down the stairs to sit down beside him.

'It wasn't bad at all at first,' Hayden answered. Emma had been such an enthusiastic help in setting up the surprise for Jane,
he hated to disappoint her, too. 'We talked
and laughed, just like when we were on our
honeymoon. We danced…'

'You got Jane to dance?' Emma exclaimed.

'Yes. We used to love dancing together.'

Emma shook her head. 'She won't dance at all now. Even at the assembly, when that stick-in-the-mud David Marton asked her.'

Marton again. It seemed the man could do, be, whatever Hayden couldn't for Jane. 'Marton asked her to dance?'

'Yes, but she made me do it instead. It was quite dull.' Emma thoughtfully stroked Murray's black-and-white fur where he lay on her lap. 'So what went wrong?'

'I fear I have hurt your sister too much for one dance to make much difference,' he admitted.

'Then you must keep on trying! And on and on, until she sees how much she misses you.'

Against his will, he felt a touch of something strangely like hope. 'She missed me?'

'I'm sure she does. She seldom talks about you or your life in London and she always tries so hard to be cheerful for me. But I see how sad she looks sometimes, when she thinks no one is around. Whatever happened, I'm sure it can't be so bad that it can't be fixed. You must keep trying.'

Hayden had to laugh at Emma's stubborn

certainty. Perhaps there *was* hope, if Jane truly missed him. If he could change, and show her that he had changed, maybe they could make a new sort of life.

For the first time he saw the faint, far-away light of something he never thought to have—hope.

'You know, Emma,' he said, 'I always wanted a sister.'

Emma laughed. 'And I always wanted a brother. You could possibly do well. But don't make me sorry I decided to help you.'

Chapter Eight

'Are you quite sure you feel like doing this?' Jane asked Hayden anxiously as they walked out of Barton's gates on to the lane. The drying ruts of mud sucked at her sturdy boots, but couldn't hold her down. 'Your leg…'

'It's much better,' he insisted with a laugh. 'You don't need to fuss any more, Jane. I know I'm capable of walking into the village without collapsing.'

Jane had to laugh, too. She *was* fussing, even though it was quite clear Hayden could take care of himself. For the last two days, since their dinner alone and the kiss that sent her life spinning, he had worked in the garden, cleaning flowerbeds with her between the rains. He dug through the piles of old books in the library with Emma. He played cards with her in the evenings, much to her giggling delight. He took Murray for walks.

And he drank only small amounts of wine and walked her to her chamber door every night, leaving her with a kiss on the cheek. She wasn't sure if she was relieved or disappointed by that sweet salute. Kissing, and all the delicious things that went along with it, were always the things the two of them got exactly right.

But she did know she was utterly mystified by this new Hayden. He was so attentive, so interested in what went on at Barton. He fit into their quiet life, as if he had merely been the last piece of the puzzle that needed to be slid into place.

Back in London, where every minute had been so full of wild, dizzying activity, she would never have pictured Hayden in his shirtsleeves digging about in the garden with her—and laughing about it. She always felt slightly on edge, waiting for his game to be over and the Hayden she'd come to see as a wild stranger emerge again. She waited for the moment he grew tired of them and left, never to be seen again.

Yet he was still there. And he showed no signs of leaving Barton.

Jane was afraid she was becoming all too accustomed to having him there, to working alongside him as they talked quietly of inconsequential things, and of watching him laugh with Emma. She'd only just begun to pick up the shards of her scattered life. She'd have to cry all over again when he did leave.

But today didn't look like it would be that day. The sky was overcast, but the rains hadn't started again. Emma wanted to walk into the village to see if there was anything new at the bookshop and Hayden immediately agreed to walk with them. It would be the first time in days that they had left their cosy nest at Barton and went out among other people. The village was not London, of course, but Jane still didn't know what would happen.

Emma dashed ahead of them with Murray, her bonnet dangling by its ribbons down her back. Hayden walked next to Jane, close but not touching, and they went in silence for several long minutes.

'Do you often walk into the village?' he asked.

'Not very often,' Jane answered, glad of something neutral, easy to speak of. 'We're so busy at Barton. But this is an easy walk on a fine day and Emma likes to visit the bookshop. We've been once or twice to the assembly rooms, too. There are a surprising number of fine musicians who live nearby and play for the dancing. It's not a grand London ball, but most enjoyable.'

'And does Emma enjoy the dancing as much as she does the bookshop?'

'Not nearly as much, I fear,' Jane said with a laugh. 'But I try to find her what society I can.'

'Perhaps there are no worthy dance partners for her.'

'Perhaps not. But then I am not sure what she would consider "worthy". She spurns whatever young man offers her attention.'

'And do you also dance at the assemblies, Jane?'

There was a strangely intent note in

Hayden's voice, as if suddenly they weren't merely chatting. Her steps slowed as they came to the small clearing where the road split off in two branches. One led into the village, the other to an old farmhouse that was half-burned and falling in on itself. A river ran along the roadside there, out of sight down a sloping bank.

Usually the waters were placid, a fine spot for a picnic on a nice day, but now it was swollen from the rains and she could hear the rush and tumble of it over the rocks. Emma had vanished down by its waves and Jane could hear her calling after Murray.

'Of course I don't dance,' she said. 'I am an old married lady. My job is to chaperon Emma.'

'Yet surely you have friends you talk to at parties? You said you did.'

What was he really asking? Jane turned to study him, but his face was shadowed under his hat. 'A few. But not as many as you have in London.'

He gave a harsh laugh. 'I don't have friends in London, Jane, as you rightfully pointed out. I have people I know.'

'What of Lord John Eastwood? Is he not your friend?' John Eastwood had been the best man at their wedding, a friend of Hayden's from schooldays, and he was the only crony of Hayden's she'd really liked. He actually talked to her. And he seemed so sad after the sudden death of Lady Eastwood. Jane had hoped John could help Hayden after their own marriage crumbled.

'John has been in the country lately,' Hayden said shortly.

'Then what of—?' Jane clamped her mouth tightly shut on the words. She'd almost blurted out 'What of Lady Marlbury?' But she didn't really want to know if he saw Lady Marlbury.

'What about what?' he asked.

'Nothing,' she said quickly. She called for Emma and hurried on towards the village, away from the river and the burned-out farmhouse. Away from the past and her own emotions of what had happened there.

The village was a small one, just a few cobbled lanes and a green centred around a stone thirteenth-century church and the long, low building housing the assembly rooms. Even though Jane didn't make the walk in very often, everyone there knew her. And they all seemed to be out that afternoon, hurrying in and out of the shops, strolling on the shady green, shaking rugs out of windows.

Everyone called out greetings to Jane, looking curiously at Hayden until she stopped to introduce him. Then their surprise turned to smiles. Jane knew they'd all wondered about her as the months went on and she stayed alone at Barton, Lord Ramsay nowhere in evidence. No one had ever been rude enough to ask outright where he was, though Louisa Marton had hinted once or twice. But now they were all so clearly happy to see them together.

Jane was half-afraid Hayden would be bored in the village. The tension of their short conversation by the river still lingered between them, taut as a rope binding them, but holding them apart.

But he went with her into the shops, carrying her purchases and conversing affably with everyone who stopped them. He was friendly, joking, chatting about farming matters and local gossip quite as if he was deeply interested in them. Jane was astonished; this was not the Hayden she'd come to know in London. This was the Hayden who had been with her all too briefly at Ramsay House on their honeymoon, the one who had slipped away from her.

'I didn't know you had read about sheep cultivation in the country,' she said as they stepped out of the draper's and turned towards the bookshop to fetch Emma.

Hayden laughed. 'I have all sorts of hidden interests, Jane. But you mustn't tell anyone. Wouldn't want to ruin my reputation as a care-for-nothing, would we?'

She had so many questions flying around in her mind. Why would Hayden hide his true intelligence, especially from her? She opened her mouth to ask him more, but suddenly a woman called, 'Lady Ramsay! Lady Ramsay, how lovely to see you again.'

Jane turned to see Louisa Marton rushing towards them across the street, the plumes on her bonnet waving. David Marton walked behind her, more cautious.

'How do you do, Miss Marton? Sir David?'

Jane said. She remembered Hayden's irrational jealousy when he had arrived at Barton and found the Martons there. How he had asked her so closely about Sir David and her 'friendships' in the village. She glanced up at him from under the brim of her straw hat, but his face was blandly polite. Only the slight narrowing of his eyes as he looked at Sir David showed he was thinking anything at all. 'You remember Lord Ramsay?'

'Oh, of course we do,' Louisa said with a giggle. 'Don't we, David? It's no wonder we haven't seen you in a few days. You two must be very busy.'

'There is certainly much to be done at Barton, Miss Marton,' Hayden said. 'I'm very grateful my wife has had such good friends to help her while I've been away on business. I wouldn't want her to be lonely.'

'Anyone would be honoured to stand in as a friend to Lady Ramsay,' David said quietly. 'Especially when she is most in need of one.'

The two men stared at each other in a long, tense moment as Louisa giggled and Jane tried to think of something—anything—to say. Finally the strange atmosphere was broken when Emma came hurrying out of the bookshop and they turned towards home after making their farewells to the Martons.

'We shall see you soon, I hope, Lady Ramsay!' Louisa called after them. 'I will have a small musical evening soon, which I do hope you will attend…'

'What did the Martons want?' Emma asked as they walked back past the burned-out farmhouse. 'Sir David looked positively animated there for an instant, which is more than I can usually say for him.'

'Don't be rude, Emma,' Jane chided. 'The Martons have been very kind to us.'

Emma shrugged and went on to chatter about the new books she had found all the way to the gates of Barton Park, so that Jane and Hayden could say nothing to each other. Jane thought that was just as well, since she wasn't sure what she would want to say, anyway. Once they were on the pathway to the house again, Emma ran up the drive ahead of them and they were alone for a moment.

'So the Martons are proud to be your good friends?' Hayden asked quietly.

'I told you,' Jane said, exasperated by his

strange attitude. 'They are near neighbours and Sir David is widely read and has many interesting opinions, even if Emma does think him dull. So, yes, they are friends. Did you think I would just sit here alone while you ran about London? That I would make no life for myself and my sister?'

'You never had to be alone, Jane. We could have shared the life in London. You could have had friends there.'

She shook her head, suddenly so tired. This was something they had quarrelled about before and there was no solution. No moving back or forwards.

Suddenly Emma gave a shout, and Jane saw her dashing back up the drive towards them, 'Jane, come quickly! It's the most amazing thing.'

Bewildered, Jane hurried after her sister until they turned the corner in sight of the house.

It really was the most amazing thing. There was *work* being done on Barton. There were several men climbing about on the roof, busily fixing the patches that had been worn away in all the rain. Others were examining the cracked windows and hauling barrows of debris from the garden.

'What is this?' she cried. She spun around to face Hayden as he limped closer to her. 'Did you do this?'

He gave a sheepish smile. 'Surprise, Jane. I thought you might be tired of moving those buckets around every time it rains.'

'Hayden,' she said slowly. She could hardly credit what she was seeing right before her— and that Hayden had thought of this all on his own. 'I—shouldn't let you do this. It's too much.'

'Of course you should. You've let me into your house; you won't take money from me. I want to do something for you and for Barton Park. Patching the roof is the least I can do now.'

He wanted to do something for Barton? Jane was amazed and touched. Against her will, she felt herself softening towards him just the tiniest bit. She'd seen a side to him today she hadn't in a very long time, and it made her feel reluctantly—hopeful. Maybe Barton did have the power to change people.

'Well,' she said, 'if you insist on patching the leaky roof, who am I to deny you?'

Hayden laughed and took her arm to walk with her towards the house. 'Now you are coming around to my point of view, Jane. I knew you would eventually...'

Chapter Nine

'Are you quite sure you don't mind helping me find books, Hayden?' Emma asked, her voice muffled from where she knelt under a haphazard pile of volumes.

Hayden smiled down at the top of her head, the straw crown of her bonnet just visible. 'Of course I don't mind. Why should I?'

Emma handed up two books for him to hold. 'It just doesn't seem like a little village bookshop would be your natural habitat.'

Hayden studied the store, the jumbled shelves jammed with volumes, the streaked windows, the old, white-haired proprietor, Mr Lorne, who obviously knew Emma very well as he had kept back a stack of books for her. It was quiet and overly warm, smelling of lavender and book dust, its own little world. 'It's true I'm not much of a reader. But I fear I would have been in your sister's way while she made the grocery order and I don't think I should try to get in her black books any more than I already am.'

'Hmm—not much of a reader. Nor much of a country dweller, I would say,' Emma said. She handed him another book and rose to her feet, brushing the dust from her skirts. 'Have you always lived in town?'

'When I was a child I lived at Ramsay House with my parents, but I don't go there often now,' Hayden answered. 'I suppose I do prefer city life.'

'Really? Why?'

Hayden shrugged, still not quite used to his sister-in-law's forthright, curious nature. It was so unlike anything he had ever known in his own family. He also wasn't used to looking too closely inside himself, the dark corners and cobwebbed passages. 'I like to keep busy, I suppose.'

'And there isn't enough to keep you busy at Ramsay House? Jane said it was quite vast.'

'So it is. And I have an excellent estate manager to keep it going for me.'

'It's not quite the same as taking care of it yourself, is it? Not if it's home, as Barton Park is. I missed it so much when we were gone from it.'

'I'm not sure Ramsay House is much of a home,' Hayden admitted, surprised to find himself saying words he had barely even thought before. But there was something about Jane's innocent sister, about the whole intimate world of Barton and its environs, that forced him to be honest. 'I never felt I really belonged there until Jane was there with me.'

Emma's eyes widened. 'But then why—?'

She was interrupted when the shop door opened with a tinkle of bells and someone called her name. As she hurried to greet her friend, Hayden moved to a quiet corner behind a bank of shelves. He pretended to examine the books, but in his mind he was suddenly back at Ramsay House. With Jane.

He had a flashing memory of carrying Jane over the threshold, the two of them laughing. Jane's laughter as she wrapped her arms around him and sent them both tumbling to the bed. The taste of her skin under his lips, the sound of her sighs. There, in bed, when they were alone, he could make her happy.

It was only when they left their sensual cocoon that he couldn't decipher what she really wanted.

Hayden stared at the rows of volumes before him and wished there was a book that could tell him, finally, what to do for Jane. How to make things right.

He heard an echo of merry laughter and, for an instant, thought it was another memory of one of their too-brief moments of happiness. But then he saw that Jane stood outside the shop window, chatting with someone, laughing at some joke. She looked as she had in those days when they dashed together through the gardens at Ramsay House, her face alight with joy, young and free.

But this time he wasn't the one to put that happiness there. Hayden had the sudden, terrible realisation that he had always let Jane down. He had swept her off her feet because he wanted her so much, then he hadn't known how to keep her. He hadn't even tried and he had no one to blame but himself. His parents had taught him badly and he hadn't even thought to escape them.

It was he alone who hadn't been the right husband for Jane. And that thought struck him like a shotgun blast.

Jane glanced through the window and saw him watching her. Her laughter faded and a frown flickered over her face. He had to prove himself to her, that was all. But how could he do that, how could he make it up to his brave wife, when he didn't know where to start?

'Hayden, you are dreadful! You must be cheating,' Emma cried as she tossed her cards down on the table. 'That is the third hand you've won tonight.'

Jane had to laugh at the disgruntled look on Emma's face. Her sister loved to play cards, but Emma was also easily distracted and often lost track of the game. She could only keep up with an experienced gamester like Hayden for a short while.

But Hayden never let Emma feel like he

was 'letting' her win, or like she was slow-witted for losing. The two of them seemed as if they could play for ever, something Jane would never have expected. But then Hayden wasn't behaving at all as she would have once expected.

Hayden grinned as he gathered up the scattered cards. 'A gentleman never cheats, Emma. Luck is with me tonight.'

'Luck is always with you,' Emma grumbled. She turned to Jane and added, 'It's most unfair, isn't it, Jane?'

Jane plied her needle carefully through the linen she was mending. 'Life is always most unfair, Emma dear.'

'Indeed it is. I wish the rain would stop,' Emma said. They could hear the drops pattering at the sitting-room window. It had started when they sat down to dinner, a slow, steady drip that would make the already muddy roads even more impassable.

So Hayden would have to stay even longer.

Jane studied him as he shuffled the cards and dealt them between him and Emma again. They hadn't spoken much since their quarrel in the village that afternoon, but he seemed to be in a good humour again. He'd laughed and joked over dinner, making Emma giggle with tales of London gossip. Everything was so comfortable between them all tonight, cosy almost.

Once, this had been all she longed for with Hayden. A happy family life for the two of them. It was the one thing he couldn't give her in the end—the one thing they couldn't give each other. To see it before her now made her heart ache at how bittersweet life could be. Emma was right—things were most unfair.

Jane had been angry at his too-quick assumptions about David Marton, that was true. Hayden had no right to say such things to her when he was no doubt engaged in all kinds of debaucheries in town! But now, wrapped up in this warm evening, she couldn't hold on to her anger any longer.

Especially when they hadn't needed to get out the buckets to catch the drips from the old roof, thanks to his efficient workmen.

'One more game, Emma, then off to bed,' Jane said, twisting the needle through the cloth.

She expected an argument. Emma was a night-owl who could happily stay up until dawn. But Emma just nodded and gave a strangely sly smile as she studied her new hand of cards.

'Of course,' Emma said. 'I have some notes to make on my new plant specimens, anyway. You can take my place at cards, Jane.'

Jane shook her head. 'I don't play cards any longer.'

Hayden shot her a quizzical glance, but he didn't say anything until the game ended and Emma bid them goodnight. Once she had left, Murray trotting at her heels, the room seemed deeply quiet. She could only hear the soft slide of the cards between his fingers, the fall of the rain, the rustle of the linen under her needle. But she was intensely, burningly aware that he sat just across the room from her. That he watched her.

'You don't play cards?' he said suddenly, the words tossed out into the heavy silence. 'I remember you were a wicked opponent at whist.'

Jane shook her head. 'I even had to give

up such old-fashioned games. I hated losing far too much and Emma has become too good a player.'

'Emma is certainly an enthusiastic opponent,' he said. 'But are you sure you didn't stop because of me?'

Startled by his stark question, Jane dropped her mending to her lap and stared at him. He looked back at her, unwavering, unblinking, his blue eyes dark and solemn. 'I— Well, yes. I didn't like what you became when you played deep in the card rooms. So intense, so—feverish. It was as if I didn't know you there. But then again…'

Her words stuck and she shook her head again. She was so accustomed to stuffing her true thoughts and emotions down deeper and deeper, so deep that Hayden couldn't see them and thus hurt her even more. She didn't know what to do with this new Hayden, this still, watchful, serious Hayden.

'Then again—what, Jane?' he asked.

'Then again, I often felt like I didn't know you at all,' she admitted. 'When I saw you at balls, in the card rooms, with your friends, I was sure I had only imagined the man I thought I married. He vanished so utterly and you never seemed to know me at all.'

He nodded and stared down at the pack of cards in his hand. A straight, frowning line creased between his eyes.

'I should have come here when you asked me to,' he said.

'What?' Jane said in surprise.

'That last night, before you left London, you asked me to come here with you and Emma for a holiday. I should have done it.'

Jane couldn't believe he even remembered that. He'd been so foxed that night on the stairs, she'd been so sure he remembered nothing about it. And when she left the town house the next day without a word from him, she was sure she was right. That he didn't care at all.

'Barton is a special place, isn't it?' he said. 'I've never felt like a house could be this way.'

Jane knew that very well. Barton was her home. But she would never have thought he could see it. 'What way?'

'Like a real home,' he said simply.

Jane's heart pounded at those stark words.

That was what she had tried to tell him so long ago; why she tried to get him to come here with her. Why did he see now, when it was too late?

She tried to laugh, but the sound came out all choked. 'Perhaps it will be, now that you have fixed the roof.'

'That was the least I could do. I owe you so much, Jane, and yet you won't accept anything from me.'

'You don't owe me anything, Hayden,' she said. She didn't want debt between them, not any longer. She'd only wanted to leave him, leave the mistake of *them,* behind so she could find some way to move forwards. But all that effort was shattered when he showed up here.

'Your family must have been so happy here,' he said. 'You never talked about them, except for Emma.'

'You never spoke of your family, either.'

His lips twisted in a strange, bitter little smile. 'My family isn't really worth talking about. My parents were most typical of the aristocratic sort. Nothing worth analysing.'

Jane had to laugh. 'My parents weren't typical at all.'

'Then what were they like?'

She closed her eyes and pictured them as they had once sat in this very room. Her father huddled over his books, her mother's lips pinched tightly together as she watched him. Baby Emma playing with her blocks by the fire. Barton Park fading and crumbling around them even back then. But there was also that sense of security and belonging, that sense she wanted to bring to her own family.

'They were—eccentric,' she said.

'That sounds intriguing. Eccentric in what way?'

'Well, did I ever tell you the tale of the Barton treasure?'

Hayden laughed and, despite everything, she still revelled in that sound. 'Treasure? Not at all. I can't believe you kept such a thing from me. It sounds positively piratical.'

'And if anyone likes all things piratical, it's surely you,' Jane said with a laugh. She told him what she knew of the Barton Park treasure and how it was lost in the mists of time.

'But even though that was a mere legend,'

she ended, 'it captured my father's imagination when he was a boy. And by the time Emma and I were older, it completely took over his life. He spent days and days poring over old family papers looking for clues and maps. My mother hated his obsession, hated how it took over everything else. My father just said she would be glad once he found the treasure and we were all rich.'

She glanced up to find Hayden watching her closely, his chin propped on his palm.

'I take it he never found it,' Hayden said.

'Obviously not.' Jane waved around at the shabby room, the faded wallpaper peeling at the edges and the mended curtains. 'He died before he could even find a real clue, while I was still a girl. My mother followed soon after, probably in a fit of rage that he had escaped her without leaving the promised treasure. That was how I came to be in London, with an aunt I hardly knew and who wasn't best happy to be suddenly saddled with two nieces.'

'And then you met me.'

'Yes,' Jane said, remembering the bright, perfect dream of that time she had found

Hayden. 'And that is the strange, sad tale of my family at Barton Park.'

'Sad?' he said. 'It's an odd one, no doubt. Eccentric, as you said. But was it sad? Were you unhappy here?'

'Not at all.' Jane was surprised at the truth of those words, at realising why it was she had longed to come back to Barton. 'Anyone with a conventional life would have thought we must be most unhappy, but Emma and I never felt so. We had a freedom most girls never know and we were always sure we belonged here. That we belonged to each other.'

'I was always quite sure I did not belong at Ramsay House,' Hayden said. Despite the simple sadness of those words, his tone was calm and matter of fact, as if everyone's life was like that.

She knew so little about Hayden's family. His parents were long dead when she met him and he never spoke about them. At Ramsay House she'd seen their portraits, but all she could glean from them was that his mother had been a beauty with her son's blue eyes and his father was very stern and unsmiling.

When she asked Hayden about his childhood, all he would say was, 'It was most typical.'

She knew *typical* for a young man of his station meant tutors and school. Not the slightly chaotic and shabby life she and Emma knew here at Barton. But what was it like when he was with his parents?

'What was life like at Ramsay House?' she asked.

Hayden shrugged. 'Quiet most of the time. My mother was seldom there; she preferred town life.'

Like her son? Maybe that was why he was the way he was. 'And your father?'

'A countryman through and through. He was most happy with his horses and dogs, or when he was walking the fields or visiting tenants. Ramsay House was everything to him. Duty and the family name, all that. I was a disappointment to him all round.'

'How could you possibly be a disappointment to them?' Jane cried. 'A handsome, popular young heir. What more could they want?'

'My brother, I suppose.'

'Your brother?' She was shocked. She'd never heard of any sibling before.

'Did you not know I had an older brother? He died as a child, before I was born, But my father was quite convinced he would have been the perfect heir. Serious and dutiful, dedicated to all things Ramsay. Not an irresponsible gadabout like the son they were stuck with. I finally ceased to go to Ramsay House on my school holidays, just so I wouldn't hear the same conversation all over again. John Eastwood's parents kindly took me in instead. Then I only had to hear about my shortcomings in letters. It all worked out very well.'

He sounded joking, as if he were merely recalling amusing peccadilloes from the past, but Jane knew him too well to be fooled. She had come to sense that there was something he hid deep inside, some hurt he covered up in drink and parties, something he would never reveal to her. Until now.

Jane's heart ached as she turned his words over in her mind. It ached for the boy he had once been, who surely only wanted to be accepted in the role he had to play. But when nothing would satisfy his father, when nothing could compare to a boy who was dead...

What else could he do but close off his heart? Live up to their low expectations until they became the truth. Until neither he nor anyone else could tell where the ruse ended and the real Hayden began.

'I'm so sorry, Hayden,' she said. 'They were wrong to believe those things. If only they could have seen the earl you've become.'

Hayden gave a bitter-sounding laugh. 'They would be just as disappointed as ever. My father would be happy to proclaim he was right, though I certainly get my taste for brandy from him. And my mother died in childbirth, trying to give my father another son long after she should have ceased bearing children. Poor Mother. But did I not disappoint you, too, Jane? In the end.'

She shook her head, her eyes aching with tears. Just in those few words she had learned so much, saw so much. Her sweet Hayden. How she missed him, missed the man she'd fallen in love with and first been married to. How deeply she wished he would come back.

Yes, she had been disappointed once. She

had been confused and angry. But now she perhaps had the first inkling of why. She didn't know how to tell him that. She had to show him.

Jane feared she would start crying at his words. Hayden tried to make them sound light, inconsequential. But she'd never heard him say much about his family before; she'd only known they had died before she met him. And now she could hear the old, but still raw, pain in his voice. The pain that told him he could never build a real family. She slowly rose to her feet, went to kneel beside him and took his hand in hers.

His eyes widened in surprise. Before he could say anything, before she could remember everything that lay like a gulf of hurt between them and change her mind, she rose up to kiss him. She pressed one swift, soft kiss to his lips, then another and another, teasing him until he half-laughed, half-groaned and pulled her even closer against him. So close nothing could come between them at all.

He moaned against her lips and deepened the kiss, his tongue lightly seeking hers, and Jane was lost in him all over again. The way it once was, the hot need that always rose in her when he touched her, surrounded them all over again like a wall of flame that shut out the rest of the world. She only wanted to be this close to him again, always. To be part of him and make him part of her.

She had questioned, worried, wondered for so long. Now she only wanted to be with Hayden again, to feel as only he could make her feel.

Hayden's lips slid away from hers and he pressed tiny, fleeting kisses to her cheek, the line of her jaw, that oh-so-sensitive spot just below her ear. The spot that had always made her feel so crazy when he kissed it. She shivered at the warm rush of his breath over her skin.

She laughed breathlessly and wrapped her arms around his shoulders to try to hold herself straight. She feared she would fall down and down into love with him again and be lost for good this time.

'Jane, Jane,' he whispered hoarsely, pressing his lips to her hair, 'we can't go on like this. I still need you so much.'

She rested her cheek on the curve of his

neck and inhaled deeply the wonderful, familiar scent of his skin. This had always been the one true thing between them, the way their bodies knew one another, craved one another. Said things they never could in words.

And she knew in that moment she had to let go of her fears. Silently, she took his hand in hers again and led him to the old sofa in the corner. She only wanted to feel the way only Hayden could make her feel. She wanted to feel close to him again.

She laid back on the cushions and looked up at him in the shadows. His eyes glowed and his face looked taut and intent with the desire she could tell he tried to hold back. She raised her arms up to him in a silent gesture of welcome.

'Jane—are you sure?' he said roughly.

'Shh, Hayden,' she whispered. She wanted no words now. Words only shattered the spell she wanted to weave around them. To try to repair some of the damage they'd so carelessly done.

She reached up and drew the pins from her hair, letting it coil around her shoulders. He'd always liked her hair and she watched his eyes darken as he studied her every movement. Feeling bolder, she shook her hair down her back and slowly unlaced the neckline of her gown. The cool air brushed over her bared shoulders.

'Jane!' he moaned, rubbing his hand over his eyes. 'What are you thinking now?'

'Please, Hayden,' she said. She swallowed her fear and smiled up at him. 'I want you. Don't you want me?'

'Of course I do. I've always wanted you more than anything in the world. But I—'

Whatever he wanted to say was lost when he caught her up in his arms and kissed her, passionately, deeply, nothing held back any longer.

Jane felt as if her soul caught fire. She had to be closer, closer. She pushed his coat away from his shoulders and untied his cravat. For an instant, he was tangled in his clothes and they fell together back on to the sofa, laughing. But once his coat and shirt were tossed on the floor and she felt his bare skin under her hands, the laughter faded.

Her touch, light, trembling, learned his

body all over again. The smooth, damp heat of his skin, the light, coarse hair dusted over his chest, the tight muscles of his stomach, his lean hips.

The hard ridge of his erection, straining against the cloth of his breeches. Oh, yes— she remembered *that* very well.

As they kissed, falling down into the humid heat of need, she felt his hands sliding over her shoulders, releasing the fastenings of her gown and drawing it away.

She kicked the skirt down and laughed as they slid together, skin to skin, the silken length of her hair twirling around them to bind them together. He pressed his open, hot breath to her neck and all thought vanished into pure sensation.

Jane closed her eyes and let herself just feel. Feel his hand on her hip, his mouth on the curve of her breast. She ran her hands over his strong shoulders, the arc of his back, and couldn't believe they were here together like this again. Her legs parted as she felt the weight of his body lower against her.

He reached between them to unfasten his breeches, then at last he pressed against her and thrust inside. It had been so long since they were together that at first it stung a bit, but that was nothing to the wonderful sensation of being joined with him again.

She arched up into him, wrapping her arms and legs around him to hold him with her.

'Jane,' he groaned, and slowly he moved inside her again. Deeper, harder, until there was only pleasure. A wondrous delight that grew and grew like a sparkling cloud, spreading all through her.

Jane cried out, overcome by the wonder of it. How had she lived all those years without that, without him?

Above her, she felt Hayden's body go tense, his head arched back. 'Jane!' he shouted out and his voice echoed inside of her, all around her.

And then she exploded, too, consumed by how he made her feel. She clung to him, feeling as if she tumbled down from the sky.

Long moments later, once she could breathe again, she slowly opened her eyes. For an instant, she was startled to find the familiar old room around her and not some new, enchanted glade. Hayden lay next to her, his arm tight around her waist. His eyes were closed, his body sprawled around hers in the way she remembered so well. Almost as if they had never been apart at all.

She closed her eyes again and fell back down into the sweet, drowning warmth of being near Hayden all over again.

Chapter Ten

⁓⁓⁓⁓⁓

It all appeared to be heading in the right direction.

Emma stood on her tiptoes to peer between a gap in the maze hedge. They weren't really talking, but every once in a while they would smile at each other, or touch hands as they passed a trowel or bucket. Emma found it most satisfactory to see those touches linger, the smiles grow longer.

There was something new, something harmonious, in the air today. Emma wasn't entirely sure what had changed, or even what had gone wrong in the first place, but it felt most satisfactory. She didn't want Hayden to go away, leaving Jane all worried-looking and lonely again.

Plus it distracted Jane so Emma could get on with her own work.

Emma ducked back into the maze. 'Come on, Murray,' she said, hurrying off along the pathway. She took the old journal from the pocket of her apron and carefully flipped the brittle pages open to the sketch she'd found. She was sure she was very close now. The treasure had to be somewhere nearby.

'Is your sister up to some mischief?'

Jane laughed at Hayden's wry question. 'Probably. She usually is.' She plunged her trowel into the rich, loamy soil of the flowerbeds and pulled up old, dead roots. Hayden tossed them into a bucket and reached out to pull up some more of the stubborn roots Jane couldn't reach.

It felt like a glorious morning. The sun was shining, the garden looked tidier and prettier under the light, and Hayden was with her. Best of all, he even seemed to be enjoying their quiet morning together.

'How old is Emma now?' he asked.

Jane sat back on her heels and swept her hair back from her damp brow. 'Sixteen. I know she can't run wild here for ever, but she seems to be so happy. After that school…'

'The school she hated?'

Hayden sounded so quiet, Jane wondered if he remembered their old quarrels about Emma when she wanted to retrieve her sister from the school and bring her to stay with them. 'Emma likes to be free,' Jane said simply. 'The school was suffocating her. I could see the light in her eyes dying, though she never talks about what happened there. I want to make it up to her. But I do sometimes wonder if I am doing her no favours by letting her run around here doing whatever she likes.'

'You want her to have a Season?'

'Eventually I suppose she will have to. But not with us being such a scandal. She would be cut before she even made her first curtsy.'

Hayden laughed wryly. 'You didn't consider that when you asked for a divorce.'

'I considered many things,' she said. 'I just couldn't see how we could go along as we have been. Married, but apart.'

'And what do you think now? How should we go on?'

Jane turned to face him. He looked so serious, so focused solely on her. If only it could have been like that years ago. If only she could have conquered her fears. If only he had listened to her then.

But he seemed to be listening to her now and that made the world of difference.

'I don't know,' she said simply. 'All these years I've thought of little else but us, the mistakes we made and how best to fix them. I could come up with no answers. After last night…'

'Things are different after last night.'

Different in a good way? Against her will, Jane felt a small touch of hope. *She* had certainly felt different after last night. She'd floated through the morning as if on a cloud, remembering every touch, every kiss. The way she woke up to find him gone, but a flower left on her pillow and a note asking if he could work with her in the garden today.

Yes, things were different. She could feel it, she knew it. But could she make it all last?

A tiny droplet of water hit her skin, then

another as the skies turned a pale grey above them. She took his hand and led him in silence into the house. Once they were in her bedchamber, she turned to him and stared up at him. Her heart was bursting with hope and fear. 'Oh, Hayden, I—'

But his mouth covered hers, catching her tentative words, her senses, her balance, sending them all whirling away until there was only him.

Her passion, which had been reawakened last night, rose up inside of her again. With a moan, she wrapped her arms around him as he lowered her back to the bed. His body against hers, the weight of it, felt wondrous, perfect.

Whatever else happened between them, *this* had always been so right. In their years apart, she'd tried so hard to forget him, to push away all her feelings for him. But those feelings were stubborn things and wouldn't go away so easily. And now, as he kissed her, they burst free like the rain from the sky.

Jane pushed his coat back from his shoulders and fumbled with the knot of his cravat, desperate to touch him. He drew back from her only to tug his shirt free from his breeches and loosen the placket in the front. He lifted her skirts up around her legs and she wrapped them tight around his hips. Then his body was tight against hers, his lips seeking hers. He smelled of sunshine and clean soap, and of himself, that intoxicating scent that always drew her so close.

She ran her hands over the smooth, warm skin of his shoulders above the edge of his loosened shirt. He groaned and kissed the curve of her neck as she arched her head back and revelled in the feel of his mouth on her skin.

He pulled her up against him. She opened her eyes and stared up into his eyes as he slowly thrust forwards.

Everything vanished but their skin touching, sliding against each other. She heard his harsh, uneven breath, his moan, and she answered it with her own cry. Then the pleasure burst over her and she clung to him, sobbing out his name.

'Jane!' he shouted. 'Jane,' he whispered, thrusting harder, faster, until she felt him find his own release. 'Jane, Jane.'

Just her name, but it was enough. In that moment, it was everything.

For a long time they just lay together amid the tangled bedclothes. Jane listened to the rain patter on the windows, the soft sound of Hayden's breath, and she closed her eyes to let the moment stay for as long as it could. Soon, very soon, they would have some serious matters to consider. Would they, could they, live together again? Where, and how? Could they possibly try again to have a family? She was afraid of the answers to all those questions, but she knew they would have to be faced. The past couldn't just be erased.

But not yet. Not nearly yet.

Chapter Eleven

Whack! Whack!

The sudden thundering, pounding noise jolted Jane from sleep. The whole house seemed to be shaking, as if caught in an earthquake. She shot up in bed, the sheets tumbling around her, and for an instant she had no idea where she was or what was happening.

The noise echoed away, leaving only the patter of the rain on the window and her own harsh, uneven breath. She realised she was in her own bedchamber. The lamp she usually left burning on the bedside table had gone out, but she could make out the shapes of the dressing table and the old *chaise*.

But what was that noise? Just a dream? Or was something wrong with Emma?

'If she let Murray run free again...' Jane muttered, remembering the last time Murray escaped Emma's room and wreaked havoc. She pushed back the blankets and swung her legs out of bed, only to freeze at the sound of a deep, rough male groan.

Hayden. Hayden was in bed with her.

Jane twisted around to see his black hair tousled on her pillow. The bedclothes were twisted around his waist, the faint light from the window playing over his bare skin. The whole evening came flooding back to her— his lips on hers, his body sliding over hers, the hot pleasure as she cried out at his touch.

He reached out and looped his arm around her waist. He tugged her closer, and she was wrapped up in the smell and heat of him. The familiar, arousing scents of bare skin and warm sheets, of the night that closed around them and made the rest of the world invisible.

'Where are you going?' he said hoarsely. His eyes didn't open, but he drew her closer against his body. She tried to resist the urge to melt into him, to nestle close to him and let everything else be damned. It felt so natural when they were together like this, so—right.

But she couldn't quite forget what woke her from her dreams in the first place.

She pushed against his shoulders as he laughed and dragged her closer. 'Didn't you hear that noise?' she said.

'What noise? I was asleep until you woke me with all your fidgeting about, woman.'

'How could you have missed it?' Jane said, then she remembered. 'Oh, yes. You could sleep through a shipwreck.'

'Well, we're not at sea now. It was just the thunder. Come back to bed.' He bent his head to the soft curve of her shoulder and pressed a light, butterfly-dancing kiss to her skin. His lips drifted over her, soft, gentle, as his fingers lightly skimmed over her arm to grasp the edge of her shift's short sleeve.

'It's hours 'til morning,' he whispered, his breath drifting warmly over her skin.

Jane shivered and twined her hand in his tousled hair. She nearly gave in, nearly tumbled into him, until another pounding volley shattered the quiet all over again.

It was like a sudden dash of freezing water.

Jane pushed Hayden away and leaped down from the bed.

'You see?' she cried. 'It's not thunder. Something is happening.'

Hayden fell back on to the bed with a groan. 'I don't suppose you could just ignore whatever it is and take that gown off.'

'Of course I can't.' Jane tugged her sleeve back into place and snatched up her dressing gown from the chaise. 'Barton Park is my home. I can't let it just be invaded by—whatever it is. Hayden, do get up!'

As she hastily tied back her loose fall of hair, Hayden reluctantly pushed himself up and put on his breeches. For an instant she was struck by the intimacy of the moment, of dressing together in the darkness. He moved so gracefully, so naturally, as if they did this every day.

There was another flurry of loud knocks, shaking her out of that stunned moment, and she spun away from the sight of Hayden pulling on his shirt. She stuffed her feet into a pair of slippers and yanked open the door.

Emma stood on the landing, peering down at the hall. Murray cowered at her feet, not much of a watchdog. Jane could hear now that the noise was someone pounding on the door.

'Who could it be?' Emma whispered, as if the invaders could possibly hear her.

'Probably just someone caught in the storm,' Jane said firmly. She couldn't let Emma see her uncertainty. No one ever accidentally wandered to Barton Park, they were too far off the better-travelled roads. 'I'll go down and see.'

'No, I'll go,' Hayden said as he stepped out of her chamber, the re-lit lamp in his hands. Emma's eyes widened, but she didn't really look terribly surprised to see him there.

'Stay here,' Jane told Emma, and she hurried down the stairs behind Hayden. He strode towards the door, looking calm and perfectly in charge despite the fact that he was in his shirtsleeves with rumpled hair. He always did manage to look as if he owned any room he was in and for once Jane was glad of that. Glad not to be alone.

He threw back the old bolt on the door and pulled it open. The sound of the falling rain grew louder, pouring into the creaky silence of the house. Jane stood on tiptoes to peer over his shoulder.

'Hayden, my friend! We've never been happier to see anyone in our lives,' a man shouted over the thunder. 'Devil of a night, eh?'

Even though the voice was slightly slurred with drink, Jane recognised it as Hayden's friend Lord John Eastwood, who had been the best man at their wedding. She had never minded him as much as some of Hayden's wilder friends, he was a funny, quiet sort of man who carried an air of sadness since he had lost his young wife. But what the devil was he doing *here*, in the middle of the night, at her home?

'Glad you decided to rusticate, Ramsay,' another man said. 'Otherwise we'd be trapped out on that godforsaken road.'

'Carstairs, John, what happened to you both?' Hayden said with a rough laugh. 'You look like you've been dragged to hell and back.'

'So we have,' John said. 'But don't say that too loud—there are ladies present.'

'If you can call us that!' a woman cried. 'Let us in, Ramsay, it's freezing out here.'

As Jane watched in stunned disbelief, Hayden drew the door open and five people tumbled in. At first they were an indistinct, dark blur, a tangle of cloaks and great coats and water dripping in sheets on to her floor. But then she saw it was three men and two women. They laughed and cursed, dropping their wet things carelessly. She could smell the rain, wet wool, expensive perfumes and the sticky sweetness of brandy.

'I do know that,' Hayden said, his voice a strange blend of strained affability and slight irritation. 'You all remember Lady Ramsay, I'm sure.'

The cacophony suddenly ceased, like birds scattered from a tree. The gathering turned to stare at her and Jane felt her throat tighten as the lamplight fell over their faces. She knew John, of course, and the other two men were also cronies of Hayden's, fellows he often went carousing with—Sir Ethan Carstairs and Lord Browning. One of the ladies she did not know, a little apple-cheeked blonde giggling behind her hand.

The other woman was Lady Marlbury. Hayden's former mistress, or so all the gossip said. She was as tall and gloriously, vividly beautiful as ever, despite her rain-soaked red hair. She looked as if she was about to burst into delighted laughter.

Jane resisted the sudden strong, burning urge to slap her.

'Of course. Lady Ramsay. It's been far too long,' John said, the first to recover his manners. He hurried over to bow over her cold hand. 'I'm sorry to burst in on you like this. We were all on our way back to London when our carriage became mired in the mud. Luckily Carstairs remembered that Ramsay was staying here.'

Jane swallowed past her dry throat. 'It's good to see you again, Lord John. How is your sister, Susan? She was such a good friend to me when I first arrived in London as a green country girl.'

'She is very well—just had her second child, you know. And you know Sir Ethan Carstairs and Lord Browning, of course,' John said quickly. 'And Lady Marlbury. This is Browning's friend, Mrs Smythe.'

'How lovely to see you again, Lady Ramsay,' Lady Marlbury said, still smiling. 'So kind of you to offer to provide a port in the storm.'

Jane could remember offering no such thing. In fact, every instinct told her to toss them all back out immediately. Barton Park was *her* home, *her* refuge, and they were everything she had run away from when she left London. But she knew she couldn't. Every rule of civility held her back.

She glanced at Hayden, who was studying his friends with a half-smile on his face. Was he happy to see them? Glad to have his dull country days interrupted? The warmth and contentment of the night spent in her bed, wrapped in his arms, vanished and she was so very cold. She tightened her robe around her.

'Come in, I'll fetch some brandy and get the fire started,' Hayden said, ushering them towards the sitting room.

'You'll start the fire?' Lady Marlbury said with a merry laugh. 'My goodness, Ramsay, but you *have* become domesticated out here in the wilds. What sort of upside-down place is this?'

They all followed Hayden, a laughing, jostling band who acted as if they were suddenly dropped into a seaside holiday, not stranded in a strange house—Jane's house.

Jane turned to see Emma standing halfway down the stairs, looking after them with an expression of intrigued astonishment on her pretty face.

'Emma, can you fetch Hannah?' Jane said, trying not to reveal her own stunned, uncertain feelings. 'And make cook see if she can make some sandwiches. It seems we suddenly have company.'

'Who are those people?' Emma asked, her eyes wide.

'They are friends of Hayden who were stranded in the storm,' Jane said as briefly as she could.

'Only Hayden's? You didn't know them in London?'

'Yes. I knew them.'

Emma looked as if she was aching to ask more, but she just nodded and hurried away to rouse Hannah and the cook. Murray scurried off behind her, his tail tucked down.

Jane wished with all her might that she could run off after her sister. She could already hear the loud laughter and jokes from the impromptu house party and it filled her with a sick feeling from the pit of her stomach. Her home was being invaded, just as the London house had been after they married. Already she could feel the cold tentacles of that old life, that life of fashion and lies, reaching out to grab at her again.

How could things change in only a moment like that? Jane leaned on the newel post and stared up the dimness of the staircase. When she fell asleep, she was wrapped in Hayden's arms, warmed by the most tentative and fragile of hopes. Now…

Now she just wanted to flee again. Yet if even Barton Park could be invaded, no place was safe.

Jane took a deep breath and squared her shoulders. She had her *duty*, as Hayden had often reminded her in the past. The duty of a countess and a hostess. She would see them through.

That resolve wavered a bit when she stepped through the sitting room door and saw the scene spread before her.

The cosy room where Hayden and Emma had played cards after dinner only a few hours before was transformed. The shabby sofas and chairs were pushed into a group around the fireplace. Hayden and John knelt in front of the hearth, piling up the kindling while the others shouted suggestions and jokes, and fell into fits of laughter.

Lady Marlbury rested her hand on Hayden's shoulder and leaned closer as if to examine his work. 'Really, Ramsay darling, I don't think being a chimney boy is your calling. That will never burn. You have far finer talents you should be using.'

Hayden glanced up at her with a lazy smile. 'First the fire, I think. Then...'

His hooded gaze slid past Lady Marlbury to land on Jane where she stood in the door-way. She felt utterly frozen in place, unable to turn away and unable to move forwards. She stared at Lady Marlbury's hand, resting so casually on Hayden's shoulder, and she wanted to yank out the woman's no doubt

falsely red hair by the roots. She wanted…
she wanted…

She wanted things to be completely different with Hayden. For Hayden and her.
For a few hours, she'd even imagined they
were different. Now they just felt horribly
the same.

She closed her eyes and for an instant she
was back at another house party, one where
she felt like she knew no one and wasn't
sure what to say or do. But Lady Marlbury
knew—she was standing with Hayden, her
hand on his arm, laughing up at him, making
him smile at her. Making jokes with him Jane
couldn't understand. That was when she had
realised her life with Hayden was not going
to be as she had dreamed. That he had an existence she hadn't been, couldn't be, a part of.

And when she opened her eyes she was
there all over again, but it was in her own
house now. The past rushing in to infect the
present.

'Look, I think the fire's starting,' Lord
Browning called. Everyone else turned to
the hearth amid exclamations of hilarity and
Hayden pushed himself to his feet.

He moved across the room towards Jane and it seemed to her as if everything had turned hazy and pale. A dream. Hayden wasn't real. Nothing was real.

But she was damned if she would let him see the deep sting of disappointment that had seized her heart. She held her head high and smiled brightly, just as she had done through all those London balls. Lady Marlbury was watching.

'Emma has gone to wake Hannah and the cook,' Jane said. 'We can get a few rooms ready very soon, if your friends don't mind sharing. We aren't really a large enough house for a proper house party.' She glanced over at the group around the growing fire. Mrs Smythe was perched on Lord Browning's knee, still giggling. 'But I am sure they won't mind sharing.'

'I'm sorry they showed up like that, Jane,' Hayden said quietly. 'I wasn't expecting them.'

'Of course not.'

'But I can't turn them out in the rain. John is my oldest friend.'

Jane saw that Lady Marlbury was watch-

ing them surreptitiously, still smiling even
though her eyes were narrowed. 'Not just
John, I think.'

'Jane, please. Everything was going so
well. They'll be gone as soon as their carriage is repaired, and then...'

'Then what?' Jane said, and cursed herself at the sharp sound of those words. She
couldn't let Hayden see, let him have the
power to hurt her again. She closed her eyes
for a moment, then went on, quieter. 'Don't
apologise, Hayden. This is your life. I'm glad
of the reminder. Now, you must see to your
friends. I'll go find Emma and help put the
guest rooms to rights.'

Hayden caught her hand as she turned
back towards the door. 'Jane, you must listen to me. Lady Marlbury and I—'

'Not now, Hayden, please,' Jane said. She
was tired, confused and her dignity was
hanging on by a mere thread. 'We can talk
later.'

Hayden stared down at her for a long moment. Jane dared not look at him. 'Very well,'
he finally said, and let her go.

She hurried away, but as she went that

laughter seemed to follow her like a dream phantom. 'Ramsay, darling, is this funny little place really where you've been hiding?' she heard Lady Marlbury say. 'You have been missing the most amusing parties while you've been buried here…'

Hayden stared after Jane as she dashed away, her shawl pulled tightly around her shoulders and her head held rigidly high. The laughing woman who had lain beside him in their warm bed was vanished and he had the sinking fear that she would never return.

In the room behind him he heard the loud laughter of his friends. Once he would have been with them in an instant, eager to pour the brandy and join in the jokes. To seize on the forgetfulness such revelry offered. Now he realised that was a mask he sought to hide behind and the mask was slipping away from him.

He had lost it in Jane's bed, when she touched his cheek with her fingertips and looked up into his eyes and they saw each other as if for the first time.

Something sharp and hot clawed at

Hayden and he raked his fingers through his hair. Part of him wanted to turn to his friends, grab up the brandy bottle and dive back into his old life. Part of him was desperate to do that.

But the other part only wanted to run after Jane. To make her listen to him, stay with him. *See* him again.

'Is everything all right, Hayden?' he heard John say.

Hayden slowly turned to face him. Of all the group that had shown up on Barton's doorstep, John Eastwood was the only one Hayden would call a real friend. They had been at school together, blazed their way through society together as young bucks, drank and caroused all over town until John married—and then lost his young wife within the year. John had only just emerged out of his mourning in time to stand up for Hayden at his wedding to Jane.

They had faced a great deal together. Hayden couldn't just throw him out—even if he wished he could send everyone else in that sitting room to the devil for what they had interrupted.

'What wouldn't be all right?' Hayden said, trying to give a careless laugh.

But John's brown eyes seemed to see too much. That was the price of years of friendship. 'Lady Ramsay didn't look happy to see us.'

'I could hardly toss you back out in the storm, now could I, old man?' Hayden said. He glanced past John into the sitting room, where the others were lounging around the fire, passing the brandy bottles and snickering about London gossip.

Lady Marlbury pushed Sir Ethan's seeking hand off her leg with a throaty laugh and he merely tried again to get closer to her. She tossed back the banner of her red hair, trying to play her well-worn haughty game, and Hayden wondered what he had once seen in her. Next to Jane's laughter, Jane's fresh beauty, she was nothing.

But still there was that pull of the past. The lure of things that used to help him dull the pain. Old habits, old pleasures. It never seemed to quite let him go.

'Carstairs said he met you at some inn and

you were coming here,' John said. 'I wouldn't have come if I'd known...'

'Known what?' Hayden said. He hated for anyone to know his personal business and he cursed that day he ran into Carstairs in that inn.

'That you were here trying to reconcile with your wife.'

Hayden had a flashing memory of Jane in bed with him, smiling up at him, her hair spilling across the pillows, wrapping around him. And the coldness in her eyes when she looked at his friends. 'We aren't reconciled,' he said brusquely. 'I'm merely here trying to arrange some business matters.'

John nodded thoughtfully. 'Just as you will. But I'll tell you this, Hayden, as your friend. If I could be with my Eleanor again, even for a moment, I would never waste my time with reprobates like Carstairs and Browning.'

A shriek of laughter caught Hayden's attention and he looked back to the group in the sitting room. Carstairs had given up on Lady Marlbury and was chasing Mrs Smythe around the sofa. A table overturned and laughter roared out again, even louder.

'What *are* you doing with them?' Hayden asked. 'They don't seem to be your usual crowd any more.'

John gave a humourless laugh. 'Because I *can't* be with my Eleanor. I have to take my distractions where I can. You should be beyond that now, too, Hayden.' He turned back to the sitting room. 'We'll be gone as soon as we can, I promise.'

Hannah hurried towards the door from the servants' staircase, a tray in her hands. The usually shy and scurrying maid, who he'd thought he had won over with his surprise dinner for Jane, gave him a withering glance.

'Lady Ramsay took Miss Emma upstairs, my lord,' she said. 'Before she could see any of—this. But the guest rooms are nearly ready if anyone wishes to retire.'

By Jove—Emma. Hayden had nearly forgotten his sister-in-law, so curious and alert. So young and innocent. Just one more reason for Jane to rue the day she had let him back into their home, back into their lives.

'Of course, Hannah. Thank you,' he said.

Hannah sniffed. 'Lady Ramsay also said she would stay in Miss Emma's room tonight.' She dropped a quick curtsy and scurried away.

Hayden shook his head with a wry laugh. It seemed as if, with that one sniff, the doors of Barton Park, which had just barely opened before him, slammed shut.

Chapter Twelve

It was more like studying zoology than botany, Emma thought as she watched Hayden's friends cavort around the sitting room. Plants always sat obligingly still and let one take notes, while animals would insist on wriggling about and being most unpredictable. Still, it was worth the observation.

Jane had told her last night, as they huddled in Emma's bed and listened to the unexpected interlopers stumble down the hall, that they would soon be gone and in the meantime she had to stay well out of their way. Her sister sounded again like the Jane who first brought her to Barton a year ago,

so strained and worried, her eyes full of unfathomable worries.

Emma had never wanted to see that Jane
again, and since Hayden came to Barton
there was no sign of her. Jane had started to
laugh again, to be the sister who used to play
with her and tease her when they were children. Hayden, too, was losing those haunted
shadows around his eyes. They all had fun
together and Emma began to hope maybe,
just maybe, they could all live here at Barton
and find a way to build a new family.

Hope was a pernicious thing. It came and
went so easily, and was so very fragile. A
pounding at the door could shatter it.

So Emma resolved to watch those people and see why Jane behaved so strangely
at the sight of them. Emma had promised
she would stay out of their way, but Jane
didn't know about this little hidey-hole in
the sitting-room corner, behind a screen their
mother had once painted with scenes of fat
cherubs and shepherds.

Emma slipped in there when everyone was
at breakfast and sat perched on a stool with
her notebook open on her lap. Murray lay

curled up at her feet, quiet for once. Even he seemed cowed by the sudden raucous invasion of their home.

Emma had decided to make notes as she would in any other study, but she sometimes forgot to write just from watching.

In her school, there had been girls like the daughter of a duke, the nieces of an earl and, scandalously, the illegitimate daughter of a famous theatre owner. Those girls had been wildly sophisticated and had to show off their gossipy knowledge even to an odd bluestocking like Emma. From them she heard tales of aristocratic parties, royal marriages gone horribly sour and *affaires d'amour*.

The girls' parents would have been appalled at what they really knew behind their demure, proper façades. So would Jane, if she knew what Emma had heard from them—including gossip about Jane and Hayden's own marriage. Jane's letters had always been sunny and loving. Emma would have known nothing at all about the marriage without that late-night school gossip.

So she had heard of people like this, even though, thanks to Jane's caution, she seldom encountered them. She had to watch them now, while she had the chance.

Lord John Eastwood she had met before. He was Hayden's friend and had been at Jane's wedding. Emma rather liked him. He sat apart from the others, laughing as he watched them. Despite that laughter, she could see a deep melancholy lurking in his eyes. She remembered he had lost his wife not so long ago.

Lord Browning and Mrs Smythe had no such depths. They frolicked around like a pair of puppies. *Amorous* puppies, Emma thought with a giggle as she watched Browning snatch Mrs Smythe around the waist and haul her across his lap. She kicked out with her slippered foot and knocked over a row of empty brandy bottles with a loud clatter. Despite the fact that it wasn't even noon yet, there seemed to be a great many of those bottles.

Lady Marlbury lounged on the sofa, a luxuriously embroidered shawl wrapped around herself. She was very beautiful, in a way Emma quite envied. So tall, so exotic, with that long, waving banner of red hair. She looked like an empress, a goddess, whereas Emma herself often felt like a milkmaid. But there was such a distance with that beauty, such a veil between her and everyone else.

And Emma didn't like the way the woman looked at Hayden, the casual way she touched him. It almost made Emma wish she could yank out Lady Marlbury's hair by the roots and toss her out in the still-pouring rain, since she was sure Jane never would.

Emma craned her neck around the edge of the screen to see the rest of the room. It seemed only those four were around at the moment. Jane and Hayden were nowhere to be seen, though Emma feared they weren't together. The last time she had seen Jane, her sister was hiding in the kitchen. And that other man, the handsome one named Carstairs, wasn't there, either.

She was rather disappointed about that. She had only caught a quick glimpse of him when everyone arrived last night, but it was most intriguing. He was very handsome, always with a mysterious smile on his face, always watching. Was he one of those rakes the girls always gossiped about? Very interesting. She just hoped he wasn't like Mr Milne.

She wondered who he was and what he was doing here. Unlike with Lady Marlbury and Lord John, she hadn't been able to observe him at all.

Emma bent her head over her notebook and scribbled another line. Murray cracked open one eye and peered up at her. It was clear he only wanted these interlopers gone and his house to himself again. He was accustomed to being the only one knocking things over and being noisy.

'Perhaps I should abandon botany and take up writing for the stage,' she whispered to him. 'This would make a fascinating play.'

Murray just sighed and closed his eyes again. Emma scribbled another line and was soon lost in her observations. People really *were* fascinating; one never knew what they would do next.

Except for dull people like David Marton. One surely always knew what he would do next.

'Well, well. Who do we have hiding here?'

Emma jumped off her stool, so startled

her heart pounded. Her notebook clattered to the floor, making Murray bark, and she spun around to find Ethan Carstairs smiling at her.

He leaned lazily on the edge of the screen, watching her with a wide, amused smile on his face. She'd thought when she first saw him arrive at Barton that he was handsome and in the light of day he was even more so. He could almost be a poet, with bright curls swept across his brow. He twirled a small golden coin between his fingers.

Despite all the gossip at her school, Emma hadn't really spent much time with young men, hadn't talked to them or flirted with them. With men like David Marton, she could simply lecture them about books and studies because it hardly mattered what they thought. But with a handsome young man like Ethan Carstairs, a friend of her brother-in-law whom she trusted…

Emma was utterly tongue-tied.

'You're Lady Ramsay's sister, are you not?' he asked. His words were a drawl as lazy as his pose, slow and careless. She remembered the rows of empty brandy bottles and realised he really should be as lazy as the others today. But his shimmering eyes, though slightly red-rimmed, watched her with lively interest.

'Yes,' she managed to say as she scooped her notebook off the floor. 'I'm Emma Bancroft.'

'Well, Miss Bancroft, I'm Sir Ethan Carstairs. Most pleased to make your acquaintance.'

'I know who you are,' she blurted out.

One of his brows quirked and he laughed. 'Do you indeed? That's more than I can say about you, Miss Bancroft. It's too bad of Ramsay to keep you hidden away here. You'd be a sensation in London.'

Emma very much doubted that. Everything she had heard from the girls at school told her she was exactly the sort who would not fare well in London. But the frank admiration in his eyes and his smile made her feel strongly warm and giggly, deep down inside.

'I'm too young for a Season yet,' she said. 'Besides, I like it here at Barton.'

'I can see why,' he said, all friendly ease. 'It's a most interesting house.'

'Do you think so?' Emma said, startled.

She loved Barton very much and it was indeed interesting, hiding so many intriguing secrets in its corridors. But it surely wasn't grand or stylish, as she was sure Hayden's friends required in a house. 'It's very old, with no modern comforts to speak of.'

'That's why it's so interesting,' he said. 'Old houses like this have the best stories. Ghosts, pirates and elopements, all sorts of dastardly doings lurking in their dark pasts.'

He looked so boyishly delighted in the idea of 'dastardly doings' that Emma had to laugh. He laughed with her and she immediately felt more at ease.

'Oh, yes,' she said. 'There are indeed many fascinating tales here at Barton.'

'And you must know all of them.'

'I try to write them down,' she said and held up her notebook.

'Will you write them into horrid novels one day?'

'I have thought about that,' Emma exclaimed. 'It might be rather fun to be an authoress.'

'I'm sure you would be very good at it, Miss Bancroft,' he said, still smiling. 'I think

I may have once heard a tale of Barton Park myself.'

'Really? What sort of tale?'

'Oh, the best sort. One of lost treasure.'

Emma was shocked. She didn't think anyone outside her family knew of the treasure. 'The stolen Stuart-era treasure?'

'Yes. Do you know about it, then?'

'Emma!' Jane suddenly called from beyond the screen. 'Are you in here?'

'Yes, I'm here,' Emma answered automatically. She scooped up Murray beneath her arm, trying to hush his growls as he eyed Ethan Carstairs standing there. She longed to stay and ask Ethan more about what he knew of the treasure, but Jane sounded so strained and harried that Emma knew she had to go.

She slipped past him, but before she left the cover of the screen he leaned down and whispered, 'I hope we may talk more later, Miss Bancroft. I am most intrigued.'

So was Emma. Intrigued—and flustered. She nodded and hurried past him into the sitting room. The others had left while she was preoccupied, and only Jane was there, standing in the doorway.

'Emma, dear,' Jane said softly, stopping her in her path.

'Yes?' Emma said.

'I think it would be best if you stayed in your room most of the time while the guests are here.' Jane's voice was quiet, but implacable. She didn't put her foot down very often, but Emma knew very well that when she did she meant it.

But how could she observe Carstairs if she was trapped in her room?

'Of course, Jane,' she said, and crossed her fingers behind her back. Surely what Jane didn't know couldn't matter? And there were lots of little hiding places at Barton that were perfect for quietly watching…

What a pretty girl, Ethan Carstairs thought as he watched Emma Bancroft walk away with Lady Ramsay. How much easier that would make his job here at this godforsaken house.

Emma glanced back at him just before she slipped out the door and Ethan gave her his most charming, boyish grin. The one that always made his London conquests giggle and blush. Emma Bancroft was no different, despite her unpolished, country-maid looks and unfashionable clothes. She smiled and waved, as Lady Ramsay tugged her away with a frown.

Lady Ramsay had always seemed a pale, humourless thing to Ethan. He never understood why all the fashion papers were so interested in her, how she got an earl to marry her. But she certainly had a lovely little sister, one ripe for a few compliments.

He hadn't been expecting that when he came to Barton with half-formed plans of treasure hunting. He only knew his allowance was soon to be cut off and he needed a lot of money however he could get it. But the fact that pretty Miss Emma already knew about the legend of the treasure, and was willing to tell him about it in the bargain, was a rare plum. No sneaking about to dig in dusty attics needed, which was good. He'd hate to muss his coat. He still owed the tailor for it.

Now if he could just entice the delectable Miss Emma into the garden for a little treasure hunting, all would be set. Two birds with one stone, so to speak.

'Why are you smiling like that, Sir Ethan?' he heard someone say.

He turned to find Lady Marlbury watching him. She was a rare beauty; even golden little Miss Emma paled next to her. But she had pushed him away over and over again.

What would she think of all her rejections once he was rich as Croesus? Would she rue them, pine for him? The thought made him smile even more and her eyes narrowed.

'I'm having a good time, that's all,' he said. 'Aren't you?'

'In a ramshackle house in the middle of nowhere, with endless rain and nothing to do?' she said. 'I don't know why you suggested we come here.'

'Because it was the nearest house, of course,' Ethan said, thankful once again for that rare stroke of luck. Luck—and a light hammer to the carriage wheel. 'I would have thought you'd enjoy the time to be with Ramsay again. Weren't you two something of an item?'

A dull red flush touched her sharp cheekbones. 'With his wife looking on? Don't be silly, Carstairs. Besides, Ramsay and I broke apart long ago.'

Ethan remembered Lady Ramsay's frown, the unhappy way she had studied them all since their arrival. 'Perhaps you'll have another chance with him soon enough,' he said dismissively, starting to turn away. He had treasure to seek.

'You should leave that girl alone,' Lady Marlbury called after him.

Ethan paused, his interest piqued. Lady Marlbury had noticed his talk with Miss Bancroft? 'Who do you mean?'

'That pretty little Miss Bancroft, of course. She is far out of your league, Carstairs.'

'Is she now?' Ethan shot a grin back over his shoulder at her. 'Who should I turn my attention to, then? Someone like you, perchance?'

She laughed, a sound that said all too clearly 'don't be ridiculous'. It made that anger surge up in him all over again.

'I'm only offering a bit of advice,' she said. 'If you mess about with that girl, you'll have

Ramsay to contend with. And you know very well you are no match for him.'

Her words echoed in his head and, as he looked at her little smile, his anger grew and expanded like one of the storm clouds outside. How often had he heard those words? No match for his father, no match for his perfect older brother, for his so-called friends. Ethan had had quite enough of it.

He'd watched Ramsay do whatever he liked with whomever he liked in society, seen him carried along by his looks and his position and his easy fortune, for too long. Those days were over. And Ethan would use Emma Bancroft to help him end them. His own time was coming, very soon.

'We'll see about that,' he said to Lady Marlbury, and spun around to stalk away. Her laughter followed him, but he knew that soon she wouldn't dare laugh at him any more.

Chapter Thirteen

Hayden leaned his head on the back of the dining room chair and stared up at the ceiling as his friends laughed and shouted around him. The dinner table was littered with empty wine bottles, many of which he'd helped consume. He felt the familiar sensation of heat and blurriness, of the devil may-care-ness that alcohol used to bring him, and yet he felt strangely removed from the whole scene. As if he was someplace else entirely.

Or perhaps he only wished he was someplace else.

He squinted up at the ceiling and saw to his surprise there was a fresco painted there. A scene of a god's dinner party, surrounded by laughing cupids and pretty girls in filmy classical draperies, darkened with smoke, peeling at the edges, but still very pretty.

Hayden felt a faint stirring of interest as he thought how much Jane would like it if he had it restored. One more piece of their home brought back to life.

Their home, *Blast it all*, he thought in a sudden burst of energy. Barton Park wasn't his home; it couldn't be. It didn't matter how he'd felt since he came there, didn't matter how the rare peace of the place had crept over him and how every minute with Jane he wanted to be with her more. This wasn't his place because he hadn't earned it and didn't deserve it. Not after how he treated Jane in London, how he refused to listen to her and tried to go back to his old ways.

He'd wanted to change when he saw her again, but he could tell she didn't believe him. That she saw his London life and thought it still had a draw on him. Now that life had come back to them, into Jane's own house. He had a few drinks, a few laughs, and he felt himself slipping back to his old ways like he was tumbling over an icy cliff. It felt just as perilous, just as unavoidable.

He sat up straight and looked out at his friends, everything slightly fuzzy at the edges from the wine. They were falling and tumbling from their chairs, shrieking with laughter over a story Browning was telling about an actress and some elderly *roué* trying to recapture his naughty youth. All except Lady Marlbury, who was only smiling distantly and occasionally giving Hayden a worried glance.

Surely he was really in trouble if even his former mistress looked at him in concern.

Once he had relished such a life. The drinking, the fighting, the laughter had made him forget everything else. Taken him out of himself. When these people showed up on the doorstep and he decided to let them in and give them the last of Jane's father's wine cellar, he'd thought maybe he could recapture some of that. That perhaps his new need for Jane could be rooted out.

Instead he only felt like he was in danger of becoming the old fool in Browning's story. He found he wanted Jane more than he'd ever wanted the forgetfulness of dissipation. And that revelation hit him like a thunderbolt.

Suddenly, the dining room door banged open and Jane stood there. Her eyes blazed and her lips tightened as she swept a glance over the party. Hayden half-rose to go to her, to tell her what he'd realised, but he fell back to the chair, words lost. It seemed he'd consumed more wine than he realised.

And the burning look she turned on him told him clearer than any words that she didn't want any apologies or excuses from him now. His wife was quite, quite angry. And she had a right to be.

Nothing had changed at all.

Jane stood on the staircase landing, staring down at the flickering night-shadows in the hall as she listened to the sounds flowing up from the dining room. Shrieks of laughter, shouted curses, the ebb and flow of talk, the clink of glasses. The sound of a bottle shattering. It had only been a day since Hayden's friends had arrived at Barton, but it felt as if her house had never been her own at all.

The three years she had spent here,

searching inside herself to find out what she wanted and how she should best move forwards, faded and she felt like Lady Ramsay of London again. Smiling, outwardly so serene, while she watched her husband break all her hopes. She'd run away from all that, willing to be alone, to be lonely, rather than let Hayden pull her down with him.

But then she let him back in, let him touch her heart again. She had let herself hope he could be what she once thought he was, that she once hoped they could be. Had she been a terrible fool?

Jane leaned on the railing and closed her eyes as she thought about those precious days here at Barton. Hayden working with her in the garden, lying in bed with her at night, talking so easily, as if nothing had come between them. Hayden laughing with Emma, bringing in the workmen to fix the roof.

Hayden holding her as they made love, more tenderly, more passionately, than they ever had before.

Jane curled her fists hard on the banister, holding on fiercely. No, she had not been imagining it all. These days had not been some mere fanciful dream. Hayden told her things he never had before, things about his family, his past. He had let her see him, as she had let him see her. She couldn't just let that go, couldn't let her pain and her anger drive her to run away as she once had.

This was her house, damn it all. And Hayden was her husband, whether he liked it or not.

But that didn't mean she couldn't be furious about what was happening down there in the dining room. Especially when she heard the sound of breaking glass again and a trill of musical laughter that could only be Lady Marlbury's.

Jane tightened her shawl over her shoulders and marched down the stairs. Hayden was behaving wretchedly and it had to stop now. She wouldn't let him vanish into his wild ways again. And she would not let her house be destroyed when it was just beginning to be repaired.

The dining-room door was ajar and she pushed it open to find a scene of chaos. Dinner was hours ago. She knew because she had turned down Hayden's invitation to eat with their guests and dined with Emma in her room instead, lecturing her sister about avoiding the wrong men.

Emma had begged to be allowed to go downstairs, just for a little while, just to 'observe'. The strangely eager look in Emma's eyes when she asked to go was yet another reason for Jane to want to take back her house. She didn't want her sweet, naïve sister talking to these people, especially not to Ethan Carstairs. Emma had been much too quiet and daydreamy ever since Jane caught her behind that screen with Carstairs.

A loud clap of thunder rumbled overhead, shaking the house. Everyone in the dining room laughed even harder and raised their glasses as if to toast the storm.

The table was covered with the remains of a hastily concocted dinner that had no doubt cleaned out the cook's pantry, a tangle of platters and empty bottles. Lord John Eastwood was not there. He had always been the most sensible of Hayden's friends. Mrs Smythe perched on Lord Browning's knee, as she so often seemed to do, and Carstairs was pouring out a glass of wine. Some of it spilled out on the table. His hair was rumpled and his cravat loosened, but he didn't look quite as dishevelled as usual.

Unlike her husband. Hayden was slumped in his chair at the head of the table, his forearms braced on the table with a brandy bottle between them. His cravat dangled loose and his waistcoat was unfastened. She couldn't see his face; his black hair was tangled over his brow. He idly twirled the bottle between his palms as if fascinated by the movement.

Lady Marlbury leaned close to him to say something quiet in his ear. An instinctive flare of jealousy rose up in Jane, but even through that haze she saw that Lady Marlbury didn't look flirtatious or triumphant. She looked—concerned.

Jane shoved the door open harder, letting it bounce off the wall with a loud bang that caught everyone's attention. Browning and Carstairs scrambled to their feet, Browning's sudden movement nearly knocking Mrs Smythe over. Lady Marlbury's hand slid away from Hayden's arm and Hayden himself looked up slowly. His blue eyes were slightly reddened, his movements careful as if not to jar an aching head.

Jane's stomach clenched as she remembered her last night in London. Hayden falling asleep on the stairs after a long night out, not listening to her when she was so desperate. So shattered.

She had to be stronger than that now.

She strode into the room, ignoring everyone but her husband. As she came closer, he braced his palms on the table and pushed himself to his feet.

'Jane,' he said roughly. 'So kind of you to join us. Have a brandy?'

Jane took a deep breath, forcing herself to stay calm. She wanted no scenes, not here. Not in front of these people. 'It's very late, Hayden. Shouldn't everyone retire?'

'Late? The evening has just begun,' Hayden said, waving his arm in a wide circle. He stumbled and would have fallen over the table if Lady Marlbury hadn't caught his arm.

'Lady Ramsay is quite right,' Lady Marlbury said. 'It is late and we have trespassed on your hospitality too long.'

She was the last person Jane would have expected to come to her defence, to be the voice of quiet reason. But as their eyes met behind Hayden's back, she could see her own weary concern reflected in Lady Marlbury's eyes. 'Come with me, Hayden,' Jane said firmly, far more firmly than she felt. But she couldn't cry now.

'We have guests, Jane,' he answered.

'I'm sure they will understand that it's time to retire,' Jane said. 'Dinner has been finished for a long while, has it not?'

'Damn it all…' Hayden said loudly, and fell against her shoulder. She stumbled back, wrapping her arm around his waist to keep them both from falling, but Jane felt herself slipping towards the floor.

Lady Marlbury caught his other arm and held them all steady. 'I'll help you get him upstairs,' she said quietly. 'Lord John retired long ago and the others won't be any help, I fear.'

The last thing Jane wanted was to accept help from Lady Marlbury, the woman who had made her feel so small, so insignificant, from the moment she married Hayden. But

Lady Marlbury was right. No one else was in any condition to help and she couldn't get Hayden upstairs by herself. She couldn't even hold him upright.

'Thank you,' she murmured, and between them she and Lady Marlbury half-carried Hayden out of the dining room. He had gone quiet again, almost as if he had fallen asleep.

They led him up the stairs and down the dimly lit corridor to Jane's room. She hoped Emma really had gone to bed and wasn't hiding to spy on everyone that night.

She and Lady Marlbury dropped Hayden on to the bed. He rolled on to his back with a groan, and immediately his eyes closed and he seemed to tumble down into sleep. Jane had that feeling of being back in London all over again, watching Hayden after a long night out with his friends.

'Can you get his boots off?' she asked Lady Marlbury as she wrestled his arm out of his coat sleeve.

The redhead nodded and set about pulling off his boots. 'I truly am sorry we intruded on you like this, Lady Ramsay,' she said quietly. 'If I had known…'

'Known what?' Jane asked curiously. Lady Marlbury didn't sound at all like her usual bold, sophisticated London self. She brushed her loosened hair off her brow as she turned to look at the woman.

'Known that Hayden was here with *you*, of course,' Lady Marlbury said. She lined the boots up carefully next to the bed. 'He just disappeared from town and no one knew what he was doing.'

'I'm sure he would have returned soon enough,' Jane said. He had only come because of her extreme step of asking for a divorce, but she wouldn't tell Lady Marlbury that. Nor would she tell anyone about the foolish hopes she'd harboured in the last few days. 'He would grow bored here and go back to the parties.'

'Do you think so?' Lady Marlbury sounded so wistful that Jane was startled.

'Of course. Look what happened tonight.'

They both looked down at Hayden, sprawled across the bed, his glossy hair tumbled, his cheeks shadowed with an unshaved beard.

'No,' Lady Marlbury said. 'What he has grown bored with is the *ton* life.'

Was she right? Jane felt a tiny touch of hope, but she pushed it back down. She couldn't let hope worm its way back in again, making her hope things that couldn't be. 'Why would you say that? We have been apart for a long time. He could have left London and come here at any time. He lives his life there.'

'Perhaps once he did. Or perhaps he was only pretending. Hayden is a great actor, you know. He can hide from anyone, anywhere.'

Jane suddenly felt so very tired. She sat down on the edge of the bed and covered her eyes with her shaking hands. It was surely only her weariness that made her sit there in the darkness next to Hayden's sleeping body, talking to the woman rumoured to have been his mistress.

'I wish I had known that before I married him,' she said frankly. 'I believed so many foolish things then. I actually thought I could make him happy. I believed we *were* happy for a while, when what he really wanted all along was someone like…'

'Someone like me?' Lady Marlbury said, laughter lurking in her quiet, sad voice.

'Yes,' Jane answered. 'Someone sophisticated and elegant.'

'Oh, Lady Ramsay. He hasn't wanted someone like me in a very long time. Our association was very brief and over before he met you. Though I confess I wouldn't have minded if it had gone on longer.' Lady Marlbury sighed. 'I was what he thought he *should* want. You were what he really wanted. Everyone could see that when you married him.'

'Then everyone, including me, was clearly wrong,' Jane said, that weariness growing and growing until it covered her like the thick, dark clouds outside.

'Were we? I do wonder. He has been like a madman ever since you left, running so wildly from one party to another, never staying in one place long,' Lady Marlbury said. 'But I have learned one thing in my life, Lady Ramsay, and that is we can't ever run far enough or fast enough to get away from ourselves. I fear Hayden is learning that, too.'

She opened the bedroom door and paused

there to add, 'I will leave tomorrow whether it's raining or not, Lady Ramsay. It's clear you and Hayden have matters that must be settled and I can't interfere. But if I may offer one bit of advice...'

Jane was completely bewildered by this whole conversation, one she would never have imagined having with this particular woman before. 'Yes, of course.'

'Keep your pretty sister away from Ethan Carstairs,' Lady Marlbury said. 'Unlike Hayden, who only pretends to be a careless rake out only for himself, Carstairs is the real thing. And there are rumours floating around town that he will soon be disinherited by his uncle into the bargain.'

'Yes, I know,' Jane said, surprised Lady Marlbury would even have noticed Emma, let alone Carstairs's questionable attentions to her. 'He will be gone as soon as I can manage it.'

'Good.' Lady Marlbury left, closing the door softly behind her.

As Jane rose from the side of the bed, she saw Hayden's rumpled cravat hanging loose around his neck and had a sudden idea. She wanted him to tell her why he did this, why he slid back to his old ways when everything at Barton was going so well. Why he had to make her so angry, so confused.

She slid the cravat from around his neck and went to dig out another one from his valise. He mumbled in his sleep and Jane straddled him on the bed, holding his arms down with her legs. She took one hand, then the other, and bound them as tightly as she could to the bedposts as he twisted restlessly.

The effort made her tired. Even drunk and asleep he was strong. She laid down beside her husband's bound body and closed her eyes, listening to his breath turn even and deep. Slowly, darkness drifted over her and she fell down into sleep. As consciousness slipped away, she smiled and thought that if only he was awake they might have had some fun, as they once did in their marriage bed…

'Jane. Untie me. Now.'

'What…?' Jane pulled herself up out of sleep at the sound of Hayden's voice. She'd been dreaming about him, vague, silvery images of him holding her in his arms, whispering to her. Now she rolled on to her side to find that he was awake and still with her, his eyes open and bright blue, free of the vagueness of drink. But his hands were still tied.

She smiled and sat up slowly to swing one of her legs over his hips so she straddled him again. She couldn't help it; suddenly she was feeling mischievous. 'I'm so sorry, Hayden, but I had to tie you. You were drunk and thrashing around too much with your nightmares.'

'I'm awake now,' he argued, watching her with narrowed eyes.

'Are you? I'm not quite sure…' Jane slowly leaned over to kiss the side of his neck. She parted her lips and savoured the sweet-salty taste of him, the way his breath turned harsh at her touch.

His body grew tense under hers. 'Untie me,' he demanded. 'Now.'

She laughed and reached up to loosen the cords around his wrists. 'Are you sure you want me to let you go just yet? There's so much else we could do. Don't you remember, when we were first married…?'

Before she could say anything else, he

rose to meet her and his mouth swooped down over hers. Open, hot, hungry, as if he wanted to devour her, just as it had once been between them. The thought flickered through her mind that he must be still dreaming, but as always when she was with him, it awakened something deep inside of her, that flame of longing and pure need. When he kissed her, he swept her away on a river of fire, swept her away to her true self, and she moaned.

Jane opened her lips to his and drew her tongue over his. His taste filled her, brandy and darkness, and she moaned.

As they kissed, deeper, hungrier, their tongues entwining, she laid her hands flat on his hard shoulders and felt the damp heat of his skin. He groaned deep in his throat, and his passion made her feel bold. She slid her caress lower, so slowly, savouring the delicious way his nearly naked body felt against hers. So strong, so hard, so hot. *This* was what she craved, what she needed. It made her feel alive again at last. Alive as she had only ever been with him.

She traced her fingertips over his flat nip-

ples and felt them pebble under her touch.
She scraped the edge of her thumbnail over
one and he growled low in his throat. She
pressed slightly harder, hard enough to give
just the slightest edge of pain. His body shud-
dered, but he went on kissing her as if he was
starved for the taste of her.

Jane slid her touch even lower, feeling
every inch of his taut, damp chest, his bare
skin. He felt like hot satin stretched over iron
muscles and the light whorls of hair tickled
her palms. She dipped the tip of her smallest
finger into his navel before she moved even
lower to the band of his trousers.

And suddenly she felt her newfound bold-
ness, the temptress inside her, flee as his
rock-hard erection brushed against her hand.
She drew away.

'Jane, Jane—don't stop now,' he whispered
darkly.

Jane smiled. Whatever else was between
them, they still desired each other. Surely
that was something. 'Do you like this?' She
moved her hand lower and lower, a slow slide
until she covered the hard ridge behind the

wool fabric. She slid her fingers down in a soft caress until he groaned.

'Jane,' he whispered darkly. Suddenly he freed himself from the cords around his wrists and pulled her chemise over her head, tearing her hand away from him. She knelt on the bed in front him, her body naked for a man as it hadn't been in so long. Not since the last time they were together, before she lost the babies. A wave of sudden cold shyness swept over her as she remembered how she looked different now, thinner, paler.

When he just looked at her with those beautiful blue eyes, silent, she tried to turn away and reach for her discarded chemise. But his hands were already on her again and he spun her back into his arms.

'So beautiful, Jane,' he said roughly as his head lowered to her breast. 'You were always so damnably beautiful.'

Jane smiled. Yes—when he looked at her and touched her like this, that strange shyness fled, and she felt beautiful again, in a way she hadn't in so long. Desirable. Wanted, and not in that way she had felt her beauty used in gaming rooms, as a commodity, a distraction. Truly beautiful. As his mouth closed hard on her nipple, drawing her in deep, her head fell back and her eyes closed. She felt the braid of her hair fall down her back and the heat of his lips on her aching breast. She bit her lip to keep from crying out. Her whole body, which had felt so frozen and numb, roared back to burning life again.

He covered her breast with his palm, his fingers spread wide to caress her. One fingertip brushed over her engorged nipple and a cry burst from her lips. She felt him smile against her, just before his teeth bit down lightly.

She reached desperately between their bodies to unfasten his trousers and push them down over his lean hips. His hard cock sprang free against her abdomen and as she held it naked in her hand at last he groaned. His teeth tightened on her nipple before he arched his head back to stare up at her.

Jane looked down into his eyes and saw that they were burning and dark, the blue almost swallowed in black lust. She bent to kiss the side of his neck, to bite at him as he had with her. He tasted salty and sweet, intoxicating.

As she kissed him, she ran her open palm up his penis to its swollen tip. Hayden's hands suddenly tightened on her backside, his fingers digging into the soft skin as he dragged her even closer. Her hand dropped away from him and he slowly pressed the tip of his manhood against the soft nest of damp curls between her thighs. He moved up and down, lightly teasing her.

'Hayden,' she whispered against his neck.

'So sweet,' he answered, in a voice so deep she didn't recognise it. He pulled her flush against his hips and then suddenly they tumbled back together to the bed. He came down on top of her, his hips between her spread legs, his lips taking hers in another wild, desperate kiss.

Jane wrapped her legs around his waist and arched up into him. He was so large, so strong and completely overwhelming. She felt surrounded completely by his heat and power. She couldn't breathe, couldn't think. She tore her lips from his kiss and tilted her head back to try to gulp in a breath, to try to find a particle of sanity. Her hands dug into his shoulders as if she would push him away—or cling to him.

Hayden seemed to sense something was wrong. His hands slid around her waist, and in one swift movement he lay on his back with her on top of him. She straddled him, her legs tight to either side of his lean hips. He stared up at her with an almost feral gleam in those extraordinary eyes, as if he was so hungry he would devour her. Yet he made no move; his body was taut and still with perfect restraint.

Jane braced her hands on his chest, letting him support her. She slid them down, a slow, hard glide over his warm skin. He felt so tense under her caress, as if he was waiting for what she wanted to do. It made her want him even more when she saw he would give her control like that.

She reached up and released the tie on the end of her braid to shake her hair free as she smiled down at him. A muscle tightened in his jaw, but his stare never wavered from her face. She took his hands and moved them from her waist to hold them to the mattress.

She leaned down and laid her open mouth on his naked chest. His hands jerked, but he didn't push her away.

She tasted him with the tip of her tongue, swirling it lightly over his flat, brown nipple. It hardened under her kiss and she felt him draw in a sharp breath of air. She nipped her teeth over him.

Surely she would always remember this, no matter what came tomorrow. It was like a dream, a lustful fantasy before she had to go back to her real life. His taste, his smell, the way his body felt as it slid against hers— she would remember it all. This had always been so right between them.

She licked at the indentation along his hip, that enticing masculine line of muscle that dipped towards his erection. She breathed softly over the base of his penis, touched him once with her tongue and sat upright atop him again.

'Jane,' he groaned. 'How do you do this to me?'

'What do I do to you?' Jane closed her eyes and laid her hand lightly between her bare breasts. Slowly, very slowly, she traced her touch down her own body, over her abdomen, until her fingers lay over the place that was so wet for him she ached with it. She slid one fingertip downwards and then his perfect stillness shattered.

'Blast it, Jane!' he shouted. Her eyes flew open as his hands closed hard around her hips. He pulled her body up along his until his mouth closed over her womanhood just where her hand had been. She knelt over his face as his tongue plunged deep into her.

Jane cried out and grabbed on to the scarred wood of the bed as his mouth claimed every intimate part of her. His fingers dug into her buttocks as he kissed her, licked her, tasted her so skilfully. She was no longer the one in control, but she didn't even care. She only wanted his mouth on her, his touch.

His tongue flicked at that tiny spot high inside of her and she moaned. One of his hands let go of her and he drove one long finger into her as he kept licking. He moved it slowly in and out, pressing, sliding, until she cried out his name over and over.

'Oh, Hayden,' she moaned. 'How do you do this to me?'

'Just let go,' he whispered against her. 'Let go for me…'

Another finger slid into her and she felt the pressure building up low in her abdomen. He had done this to her in that warm, dusty hut, too—it didn't seem to matter where they were, who they were, only that they were a man and a woman drawn together by a deep need. That heat built and built, expanding inside her like a fire out of control. Her whole body seemed to soar upwards. Hayden's tongue pressed harder as his fingers curled inside her and she shattered completely. She screamed out loud and clutched at the bed to keep from falling.

But he wasn't done. He lifted her off of him and pushed himself up to sit against the bedpost. He drew her body down until she straddled his hips again and was spread open over him.

'Ride me, Jane,' he commanded.

She could hardly focus through her pleasure-dazed mind. She stared down at him as she held on to his sweat-slick shoulders. His eyes were still dark with lust. It made her want him, need him, all over again.

She raised herself slightly until she felt his tip nudge at her opening, then she held on to him tightly as she slid down. Lower, lower, until he was completely inside of her. His head fell back as his hands closed hard on her waist.

'Jane,' he groaned. 'You're so perfect. I can't...'

She raised up again and sank back down, over and over, faster, until she found her rhythm. His hips arched up to meet hers and they moved together, harder, faster. Until she felt her climax building all over again.

She leaned back and braced her hands on his thighs as he thrust up into her. She closed her eyes and saw whirling, fiery stars in the darkness, exploding around her in showers of green and white as she cried out his name. He shouted out a flood of incoherent curses as his whole body went rigid. She felt him go still deep inside her as he let go and soared free with her.

Jane sobbed and let herself fall to the bed. Her legs were too weak to hold her up any longer. She trembled as she let the bone-deep exhaustion claim her. The ceiling above her spun around and around as she tried to catch her breath, to make sense of what madness had just happened.

Beside her, Hayden had collapsed on the pillows. They didn't touch, but she could feel the heat of his body close to hers. His breath sounded rough and uneven, and suddenly she remembered the injuries that had brought him to her door in the first place. She sat up to frantically examine him, worry replacing the languor of sexual pleasure. Had she hurt him? What craziness had come over them to do something like that?

But he looked well enough. His leg was still bandaged in clean white linen and the cloth wasn't spotted with blood. His eyes were closed, his hair falling in damp waves over his brow. She gently brushed it back and he caught her hand in his to kiss her palm. Jane felt a sudden wave of unwanted tenderness wash over her. Tenderness—for her husband of all people! After he got drunk with his friends again! Her head was spinning, as if the reality of what had happened could hardly sink in. She had never felt quite that way before. The heat of sex and need was all tangled up with the past and she didn't know what would happen next.

She didn't even know what she *wanted* to happen next. She laid her hand gently against the side of Hayden's cheek. There was so very much she didn't know about him any more.

Jane traced the hard line of his roughened jaw and over the softness of his sensual lips. Her touch drifted over his closed eyelids and she felt his breath drift softly over her skin. His arm wrapped around her waist and he drew her down to the bed beside him.

'Jane,' he whispered hoarsely, his voice distant as if he was drifting into sleep. 'What is it that you do to me? I only feel this way with you.'

She shook her head. What did they do to each other? He made her crazy, made her forget everything else when she was with him. She couldn't let him do that to her any more.

Hayden watched Jane as she slept, half-afraid she would disappear if he turned away. A tiny smile lingered on her lips as if she was having good dreams, the worried look she wore before she fell asleep vanished. He hoped she did have sweet dreams. He hoped she dreamed of him and that for once he made her smile.

Her dark hair fell in a shining curtain over her shoulders and the pillows, just as it had in his memories for so long. He ran a gentle fingertip along one soft strand and marvelled that after so much time they were here. Together.

Careful not to wake Jane, he lay back against the pillows and gently drew her into his arms. She sighed and nestled against him, and he felt a surge of something like triumph that she would trust him enough to stay close to him.

Could he trust himself? Once, long ago, he thought he could, when he first found Jane. But then he fell back to his old ways and came to heartily regret it. Jane had been his chance and he had foolishly thrown it away. Until he saw her again, saw how life could be here at Barton Park, he hadn't even realised just how foolish he really was.

But maybe now they could start again.

'What are you thinking about?' Jane suddenly asked softly.

Hayden glanced down to see that she was awake, watching him with her wide, calm hazel eyes, though she hadn't moved at all.

'About you and life here at Barton,' he answered truthfully.

'Good thoughts, I hope,' she said.

He smiled down at her and drew her even closer. 'The best, I think.'

Jane laughed, a wonderful, light, bright sound. 'That is good.'

And then she kissed him, and he couldn't think anything at all.

'The Earl and Countess of Ramsay.'
Jane heard the words ring out before her as she waited to step into the noisy ballroom. Ramsay. It was her title now, yet it sounded foreign. Would it ever seem as if it belonged to her, as if it fit as closely as the new kid gloves on her arms?

The countess business was so very new. She still felt as she had when she jumped into the lake at Ramsay House with Hayden and the cold water closed over her head. She just

*had to do as she had then and fight her way
to the surface.*

*Hayden held his arm out to her and gave
her a puzzled glance. She suddenly realised
that, yes, Ramsay was her name and thus she
was expected to step into the ballroom now.
She gave him a shaky smile and took his arm.*

'You look lovely,' he said.

*'It is the new gown,' Jane answered. She
shook out her blue silk, lace-frothed skirts—
'The very latest from Paris,* madame,*' the
modiste had said. 'It's far grander than anything else I've worn. Except my court gown
and that was borrowed.'*

*'No, it's you. I shall be the envy of every
man here.'*

*They swept into the ballroom, which was
already crowded with people, the cream of
the* ton. *Thousands of candles cast golden
light over sparkling jewels, gleaming sat-
ins and masses of red-and-white hothouse
flowers. Every eye in the room seemed to
watch her, speculative, amused, wondering.
The burst of confidence Hayden's words had
given her faded, but she forced herself to
keep smiling.*

'Ramsay! How wonderful you could attend my little soirée. I wasn't sure you were back in town yet.' Their hostess, Lady Marlbury, hurried towards them on a cloud of expensive perfume. Tall and elegant, with dark red hair swept up into a jewelled bandeau and emerald-green silk swirling around her, she was what Jane would have once imagined a countess would be like.

'We wouldn't miss it for anything. Who could be anywhere but London when your annual ball is happening?' Hayden said. He let go of Jane's arm to kiss Lady Marlbury's hand.

'You are such a flatterer,' Lady Marlbury said with a flirtatious laugh. She tapped him lightly on the arm with her folded fan. *'But I don't mind. And this must be your new wife. I have heard so much about her, though I fear my wedding invitation must have gone missing.'*

After the pleasantries were exchanged, Lady Marlbury begged to *'steal away'* Hayden for a dance, leaving Jane to linger alone for a moment.

But she was not alone for long. Susan

Eastwood, her friend from their Drawing Room débutante days, hurried to her side, holding out a glass of wine.

'My dear Lady Ramsay,' she said. 'You look as if you could use this.'

'Thank you,' Jane said with a relieved laugh. She took a long sip and sighed. 'It is quite delicious.'

'Only the best at Lady Marlbury's ball, you know.' Susan winked at her over the edge of her own glass. 'I'm surprised you're so calm about letting Lord Ramsay dance with her.'

'I don't let *him do anything,' Jane protested. 'She's our hostess, is she not? It's only polite.'*

'Polite? Perhaps it is now. But my brother John, who as you know is great friends with your husband, said last year Ramsay and Lady Marlbury were quite an item. Not that it could go anywhere, of course. Ramsay has his title to consider.'

'Were they?' Jane whispered, suddenly feeling cold. Her gaze scanned the dance floor until she found Hayden and Lady

Marlbury, their arms linked as they twirled around, laughing into each other's eyes.

Of course she knew Hayden had had amours before they met. He had to, a young, handsome, healthy earl. Yet to see it now, right before her, with such a very beautiful woman...

'How interesting,' she murmured and gulped down the rest of her wine.

'It's just silly gossip, of course,' Susan said. 'He has you now.'

Jane had to laugh, so she would not cry. 'Yes. Now he has me.'

Chapter Fourteen

Emma twisted the book in her hands upside down and studied the map again. It was a crude old drawing, out of scale and rough, and most of the landmarks in the garden had changed since the 1660s. But she was sure, after studying it for long hours, that she had finally deciphered it.

Unfortunately, if her new calculations were correct, the treasure was possibly buried under the summerhouse there at the centre of the maze, right across from the marble bench where she now sat.

She took her notebook out of her bag and jotted down a note next to her own sketches. It would certainly make her task a lot more

difficult if that was indeed where the treasure lay. The weather wasn't making things
any easier.

Emma glanced up at the sky, frowning.
The rain had paused that morning, long
enough for Lord John Eastwood and Lady
Marlbury to depart on horseback, but the
sky was still thick and grey. The ground was
so muddy and churned-up she wasn't sure
where to start digging, or even if she should.
Maybe the treasure was better left a legend.

Or so she had thought when it looked like
Jane would reconcile with Hayden. With the
Ramsay money, and a true family, Barton
wouldn't need the treasure. But today that
all looked like a faint, foolish hope. Emma
wasn't sure exactly why, but everything had
changed in an instant when Hayden's friends
had arrived. The bright, light days vanished
and the clouds closed in around the house
again.

Emma hated it. But she didn't know how
to change it, so she had done what she could.
She came to the garden to treasure hunt
again.

A sudden rustling noise from beyond the

walls of the maze made her jump to her feet. It had been so quiet, so still, since she got there that the sound made her whole body go tense. Her heart pounded and Murray sat up straight with his ears at attention. Emma slammed her notebook shut and clutched it between her hands, as if it could be a weapon.

A head peered around the edge of the wall and Emma's breath escaped in a 'whoosh'. It was Ethan Carstairs, and only when he smiled at her did she realise she had half-hoped, half-feared to see him alone again. She'd been thinking about him too much since their brief conversation behind the screen.

'I hope I didn't startle you, Miss Bancroft,' he said, stepping into the clearing. 'I thought I heard someone in here. I was just exploring a bit.'

'I— No, not at all,' Emma managed to stammer. 'It's just that no one ever comes to the maze, so I usually expect to be alone here.'

'Am I intruding, then?'

'Not at all. I'm glad of the company.' Emma slowly lowered herself back down to the bench, watching as he came closer. He really was so handsome, just what a London man-about-town should be, in her imagination. But here, outdoors in the daylight, she could see that his skin was pale, his eyes red-rimmed with the late hours she had heard everyone having last night. 'I thought everyone was leaving today.'

'I'll be on my way later, as soon as I can arrange transportation,' he said. He sat down next to her, his legs stretched before him lazily. She could smell his cologne, something sandalwoody and exotic, with the underlying tang of brandy. 'I don't think your sister likes me very much.'

'Oh, no,' Emma cried, compelled to jump to Jane's defence. There was something about his tone she didn't care for, some kind of careless laughter overlaid by a touch of bitterness. 'She is simply used to having Barton Park to herself.'

'Are you used to being alone as well, Miss Bancroft? Do you resent the intrusion of guests?'

Did she? Emma suddenly wasn't sure. She did like the quiet days at Barton where she was free to do as she liked. Especially after the torture of school. But at first having something different in the house had been exciting and interesting. New people, new gossip, new things to think about.

Then she saw how it changed Jane and Hayden, changed the way the house felt, and she wasn't sure the excitement was worth it.

She studied Carstairs closely and he watched her back with glittering eyes.

'I don't mind guests,' she said carefully. 'Especially since I couldn't have come outside much for the last few days, anyway. I liked the distraction.'

He laughed. 'So we're a distraction, are we? And now you can come outside again you no longer need us.'

'Not exactly,' Emma said cautiously. She had been interested in Ethan Carstairs before, maybe even attracted. All she knew of attraction was from books and from that disaster with Mr Milne, and there were the daydreams, the nervousness, the breathlessness she expected. Now something was making her uneasy, something slowly creeping into the edges of her consciousness. She wasn't sure what that feeling was, but it made her ease away from him on the bench. 'I'm just glad to get back to my work.'

'Your work, Miss Bancroft? And what is that? Something in that book you always have with you?'

Emma's grasp tightened on her notebook. 'It's just something silly. About what we talked of before—old houses and legends.'

His smile tightened. 'Treasure, is it?'

Something told her not to reveal too much to him, not so soon. 'Not necessarily. I just like investigating old tales.'

'I don't think I believe you, Miss Bancroft,' he said jokingly. 'I think you are treasure hunting. Have you found anything?'

'Of course not,' Emma said, trying to laugh. She slid to the very edge of the bench, but he followed her.

'Let me see your book,' he insisted. The veneer of joviality was still there; he still smiled down at her. But now Emma could see the tight desperation at its edges and it made her chest feel painful, as if she couldn't catch her breath.

She'd thought Jane was so silly to tell her

to stay away from Carstairs, from all their unexpected guests. He had seemed so fun, so flirtatious, so—admiring. She didn't know what was happening now, but she didn't like the way it made her feel at all.

'It's just silly scribblings,' she insisted.

'I doubt anything done by a smart girl like you could be silly, Miss Bancroft,' he said. 'You deserve so much more than to be buried here where no one can see you. You should be in London, where you can be admired and appreciated. I could do that for you, if you helped me in return.'

Helped him? She didn't even want to know what that meant. 'I'm happy here,' Emma gasped as she leaped off the bench. Her notebook tumbled to the ground and Murray jumped up with a loud volley of barking.

'Let me help you, Emma, please,' he said sharply, lunging to suddenly catch her arm. He dragged her back towards him, his fingers curled tightly, painfully, around her. He dragged her up against him and cold panic flooded through her.

'No!' she cried, twisting to try to break free. How had the situation spiralled beyond her so quickly? The whole maze seemed to close in around her and Murray's furious barks sounded so far away.

His other arm closed hard around her waist and pulled her closer. His lips touched the side of her neck, wet and soft, and Emma tried to kick out at him. Her skirts twisted around her leg, making her fall backwards.

As she fell, her arm wrenched free of his grasp and she managed to roll away and leap to her feet. She ran as fast as she could to the maze entrance. Just as she was fleeing the scene, Carstairs gave a ringing, furious shout.

She glanced over her shoulder and saw Murray sink his sharp little teeth into the man's leg. He kicked out and Murray flew away with a yelp.

'Murray, no! Come with me now,' she screamed and the dog came dashing towards her, limping on his back leg. She caught him up under her arm and flat-out ran.

'You little witch,' Carstairs shouted after her. 'You'll be ruined, just like your stupid sister! I offered you everything.'

Sobbing, Emma kept running until she

reached the house. She didn't know where
to go, what she should do. She only knew she
couldn't let Jane see her like this, couldn't let
anyone see what a fool she was. Again. It was
just like Mr Milne. And Jane had enough to
worry about.

Emma heard Hannah singing and the rattle
of china from the dining room, so she ducked
down the servants' stairs to the kitchen. Cook
was hunched over the stove, her back to the
door, giving Emma enough time to slip into
a small pantry and close the door behind her.

There in the cool darkness, she knelt on
the flagstone floor and clutched Murray's
soft warmth against her as she sobbed.

Only then did she realise she'd left her
notebook behind in the garden.

Jane carefully folded a stack of linen to
take down to the kitchen, trying not to look
at the bed. But every once in a while she
would glance at it from the corner of her eye,
then bit her lip to keep from giggling at the
sight of the rumpled bedclothes and the discarded cravats she had used to tie Hayden to
the bedposts.

Every time she saw them the whole night came flooding back to her, in vivid, lightning-flash detail. And she could feel the heat flood her cheeks. She couldn't quite believe she'd done that. The Jane she was before she met Hayden, even the Jane who was his wife in London, would never have done such a thing.

But when she saw Hayden lying there foxed last night, and thought about all they could have that he seemed determined to throw away, she just felt so *furious.* So tired of it all. And having him there, seemingly at her mercy, though she knew very well he could easily escape at any time and tie *her* up instead, restored some of her balance. Made her see clearly again.

The fact that he let her do that, let her feel powerful for once in her life and not just buffeted about by the whims of everyone else, made some of her anger fade. She did still love Hayden, but if he preferred a life with his friends, a life of drink and carelessness, instead of what they could have together, she could do nothing about it in the end.

But, by Jove, she could show him what he

was missing. She could make him sorry he chose so poorly.

If she ever saw him again.

Jane sighed as she folded the last piece of linen and stacked them in a basket. When she woke that morning, early enough to see Lord John Eastwood and Lady Marlbury ride off in the mist-shrouded dawn, Hayden was gone. His clothes had been picked up from the floor. She almost would have thought the whole crazy night was a dream, if not for the creased sheets on his side of the bed, the black strand of his hair on the pillow.

His horse was still in the stable when she checked, but she hadn't seen him. She was half-afraid to go searching, afraid that in the cold light of day whatever had happened between them last night, all that wild, frantic heat, would dissipate. And she would see there truly was no hope for them.

Hope was all she had to cling to now. She only had a shred of it, but still she held on to it. She remembered what Lady Marlbury had said—Hayden had changed when he married her. It was over with Lady Marlbury before they even met. It could all be lies, of course, and Jane feared she would soon feel even more foolish, but she had to hope. Just for a little while longer.

Unless Hayden didn't show up again.

Jane gathered up the basket and carried it out into the corridor. Lord Browning and Mrs Smythe's luggage was left in the hall, waiting for their repaired carriage to arrive, but their doors were still closed, as was Ethan Carstairs's. No doubt they were still sleeping off last night's revelries. She couldn't see any of Hayden's belongings among them, so maybe he didn't plan on returning to town with them.

As Jane hurried down the stairs, she realised she hadn't seen Emma that morning, either. Hannah said Emma had grabbed a piece of bread and an apple from the kitchen before dashing off to the garden with Murray. Emma did that so often it was hardly something Jane would worry about, but with Carstairs still around…

Jane frowned when she remembered the way he had looked at Emma when she found them talking behind the screen. He looked so—speculative. And Emma looked so dazzled, just as Jane herself had when she first went to London and met the men there. Jane knew she would have to be much stricter about Emma's education from now on.

In the kitchen, the cook was slumped over asleep in her chair in the corner and Hannah was standing over the hearth, boiling a cauldron for the laundry. Even though the low-ceilinged room was too warm, and there were piles of dirty dishes and rumpled laundry to be cleaned, Hannah was humming as she worked.

'I'm afraid there will be a bit more work once all the guests are gone, Hannah,' Jane said as she put down the basket and went to make sure the drying racks were set up.

'Just as long as they go, my lady,' Hannah said. 'It will be good to have the house to ourselves again.'

'Indeed it will.' Jane just hoped Hayden wouldn't decide to leave with them. 'Have you seen Emma again this morning?'

'Not since she went out to the garden, my lady.'

'Well, when she returns be sure to let

me know at once. And if you see Lord Ramsay—'

'Oh, he's in the library, my lady.'

So he *was* still there. Jane smiled in relief. But Hayden was not exactly a bookish sort. 'The library?'

'Yes. I saw him go in there as I was carrying up the breakfast tray for Lady Marlbury.' Hannah giggled. 'He looked as if someone had dragged him through the hedgerows and back, my lady, if you'll pardon my saying so. I left a pot of good, strong tea outside the door for him.'

'No doubt he'll need it,' Jane murmured. After all that brandy, and the long hours in bed—he was surely in need of some strong tea. Which surely meant this was *not* the best time to talk to him.

Jane gathered up some jars of marmalade and pots of butter from the table and hurried off to store them back in the pantry. When she first opened the door, the light from the kitchen didn't reach its furthest corners and she blinked against the sudden dimness.

Then she heard a strange rustling sound, a sniffle and a growl. Her shoulders stiffened, as it seemed she was still on full alert after the invasion of her house.

'Who is there?' she called, hastily stashing the jars on a shelf. 'What are you doing in here?'

'It—it's only me, Jane,' Emma said, her voice small.

'Emma?' Jane cried. 'Whatever are you doing hiding in here?'

She knelt down on the cold stone floor and heard Emma slide out from under the shelves. Murray whined and a beam of light from the doorway fell over them as they huddled together on the floor.

Jane's stomach clenched painfully when she saw Emma's tearstained face and tangled hair. She looked ten years old rather than sixteen, lost and bewildered. One arm was wrapped around her dog and Jane saw bruises darkening her skin.

Jane had never felt such raw, fiery fury before in her life as she looked at her sister. She would kill whoever had done this with her bare hands. She had to force herself to speak quietly, gently, and not scare Emma further.

'What happened, Emma dearest?' she said. 'Who did this?'

'Oh, Jane, I am so, so sorry!' Emma sobbed. 'I know you told me not to speak to him and I tried not to, truly. I was in the maze and he surprised me...'

'Carstairs?' *Of course.* Jane had known the man would be trouble, had felt it in her very depths when she saw how he looked at Emma. She felt horribly guilty for not tossing him out in the rain, then and there. But he was one of Hayden's friends.

Hayden's friends—who had come here to do such things.

'Yes. He asked me about my book and I knew I shouldn't be alone with him there. When I tried to leave, he grabbed me. Murray bit him and I ran.'

'What a good dog Murray is,' Jane murmured, vowing to forgive the puppy for chewing slippers and ruining rugs. He'd protected her sister when she wasn't there.

'I'm so sorry, Jane,' Emma cried. 'I should have listened to you. I was so silly.'

Jane drew Emma into her arms and held on to her tightly as Emma's back trembled with sobs. She smoothed her sister's hair and whispered soft, gentle words.

'It's not your fault, Emma,' she said. 'You did not seek him out. You were merely minding your own business in your own house. He is a wicked man. Thank goodness you got away from him so quickly.'

After a few moments, Emma's sobs faded to sniffles. 'I won't ever be alone with a man again. Ever. I promise.'

Jane had to smile at Emma's fierce tone, despite the anger that was growing like a ball of fire inside her. 'One day there will be a man you can be alone with, dearest. A much more worthy man than someone like Ethan Carstairs. He is only a scoundrel.'

'But he was so handsome, and he—he seemed to like me. I feel ridiculous.'

'Appearances aren't everything. You know that.' And so did Jane. Hayden was *never* what he appeared to be and he always seemed to change on her in an instant.

'I won't forget it again.'

After a few more minutes, Emma sat up straight and smoothed her tangled hair. Jane handed her a handkerchief and Murray looked on worriedly as Emma wiped at her eyes.

Jane knew what she had to do. She couldn't deal with Carstairs alone as he deserved. Hayden had brought these people into Barton Park. He had to help her now.

'Better?' she asked.

Emma nodded. 'You aren't angry with me, Jane? For being so foolish?'

'Oh, Emma. If being foolish was a great offence, I would have to be furious with myself. We will both be more careful in the future.'

'What do *you* have to be careful about? You've always been perfect.'

Jane laughed. 'Come along,' she said, helping Emma up off the floor, careful not to touch her bruises. 'You could use some tea, I think.'

Once she had Emma settled next to the kitchen fire with Hannah, Murray sitting watchfully at her feet, Jane climbed resolutely up the stairs. She marched to the library and unceremoniously pushed open the door.

Hayden sat behind her father's old desk,

slumped back in his chair with his eyes closed. Her account ledgers were open in front of him, as if he had been trying to work on them, and Hannah's tea tray was pushed to one side. He didn't look as rumpled as last night; his hair was brushed and his coat was draped over the chair. But he still looked tired, as tired as she felt with everything rushing at her at once.

His eyes opened at the slam of the door and he sat up straight.

'Jane,' he said, smiling tentatively. 'The carriage is coming around to the front for the remaining guests in a moment. I was just looking at the numbers here...'

'Carstairs attacked Emma,' she blurted out. She hadn't meant to say it quite like that. She'd meant to calmly tell him what had happened and what she wanted him to do about it, but her calm was dissolving around her as she thought of Emma sobbing in the pantry.

Hayden's smile vanished and his whole face hardened. He pushed himself to his feet. 'What did you say?'

'I found Emma in the pantry, crying. She—she has bruises on her arm and she told me Carstairs grabbed her. He came across her in the garden and…'

Hayden reached for his coat on the back of the chair and shrugged into it. Everything about him seemed to have gone very cold and still in only an instant. 'Is that all that happened?'

'I think so. She said Murray bit him and she was able to run away. But…' Jane shook her head, and found that she was shaking. 'Men like that should never have been in my house, around my sister! She is only sixteen and so sheltered.'

'Where is he now?'

'I don't know. Emma said he found her in the garden maze.'

'I will find him. He can't hide from me.' Hayden paused beside her in the doorway. He reached out to touch her arm, but when she stiffened his hand fell away. His face grew even harder, as if it was carved from granite. 'This is my fault, you are right. I'll take care of it.'

'What are you going to do?' Jane called after him as he strode down the corridor.

He didn't answer, and she hurried behind

him as he went out the door into the garden. She'd never seen Hayden quite like this, so silent, so still and stony. She didn't know what had happened between last night and this morning, what he'd wanted to talk to her about when she burst into the library, but this new Hayden had her most concerned.

'Hayden, wait!' she cried, but he was too far away to hear her. His long legs had carried him across the garden paths and he disappeared into the maze.

Jane ran to catch up, chasing him down the twisting walkways. As she slid into the clearing at the maze's centre, she saw Hayden was already there. And so was Carstairs.

At first the man didn't see them. He knelt in the mud near the summerhouse, digging frantically. His coat was flecked with dirt, his hair streaked with sweat and he was so engrossed in his labour he didn't notice them.

Jane's throat felt so tight and dry that she couldn't cry out. She pressed her hand hard against her stomach as she tried to catch her breath and watched helplessly as Hayden moved as quickly and silently as a large, lethal jungle cat.

He grabbed Carstairs by the back of his coat and pulled the man to his feet. Carstairs shouted out in surprise, spinning around just as Hayden shoved him away. But Hayden wasn't done with him. He followed as the man tried to run and planted a solid facer to his nose. As blood spurted and Carstairs screamed, Hayden just grabbed him up again by the coat collar and half-marched, half-dragged him out of the maze and up to the front of the house where the carriage was waiting, with Lord Browning and Mrs Smythe already inside.

Hayden shoved Carstairs inside, watching impassively as the man fell to his knees on the carriage floor. 'Don't expect to enter the club when you return to London,' Hayden said. 'Or anywhere else for that matter. And if you ever, ever come near my family again, that broken nose will be the very least of your troubles.'

Then he slammed the door and with a slap of his palm on the carriage door sent it rolling away. Carstairs never had time to say a single coherent word.

Jane stared at Hayden, shaking with the

force of all the emotions rolling through her. His shirt was torn and a bruise darkened his cheekbone. She just wanted to take him in her arms, hold him as she cried about all the things she had seen.

But there was also a part of her, a small but insistent part, that wouldn't let her forget *he* was the one who had brought these people into her house in the first place. He was the one who drank with them, who let them break the peace of Barton Park.

It wasn't completely fair, she knew that. He couldn't really have tossed them out in the storm, any more than she could have done to Hayden when he arrived in the midst of the rain. But so very much had happened— her house invaded, the strange talk with Lady Marlbury, the intense lovemaking with Hayden, Emma being attacked and the violence of Hayden's fight. She simply couldn't make her thoughts stop spinning.

She wanted to be alone to cry, to try to think.

'I have to find Emma,' she said, spinning around to run up the stairs.

'Jane…' Hayden said and she felt him

reach towards her. She didn't want him to touch her, not now. She didn't want to shatter.

She slid away, not looking back. 'We can talk later, Hayden. I have to see to my sister.'

'Of course,' he said tonelessly.

She nodded and hurried into the house. Only when the door was closed between them and she was alone did she let herself cry.

She was so damnably tired of tears, she realised as she dashed them away. They never solved anything, not in London and not here. She still loved Hayden. And they still wanted such different things from life.

She wouldn't cry any more.

Hayden's blood was up. He knew he shouldn't go back to the house when he felt like that, as if he would lash out at anyone in his path. Especially when Jane looked at him like that, as if what had happened to Emma was his fault. Her beautiful hazel eyes so full of anger and sadness.

Or maybe that was his imagination. Maybe he was sending his own shattered thoughts on to her. She *should* blame him.

He let Carstairs and the rest of them into Barton, let them send him spiralling back into the past. Jane had given him another chance when he didn't deserve it and he pounded her kindness into the ground. Again.

His sweet, darling Jane. His wife.

Hayden paced the muddy lane, his fists curled tightly around his bruised knuckles. He wanted to hit something again, wanted to be face-to-face with Carstairs again to beat the villain down. But Carstairs was gone—Hayden had seen to it himself, had tossed the blighter into a carriage and followed it into the lane to be sure it was headed towards London.

And he could never beat down what he was most angry at—himself.

Chapter Fifteen

The sitting-room door opened, and Jane sat up eagerly, the book she was pretending to read falling from her hands, only to sink back down to her chair when she saw it was Hannah standing there and not Hayden.

The clock was ticking inexorably towards dinner time, the sky outside the window darkening, and still Hayden hadn't come back. Her anger was tinged with the sharpness of worry. Where could he have gone? Was he in trouble somewhere?

She hadn't liked the wild light in his eyes when he tossed Carstairs out of the house. She'd seen that look too often and she didn't want yet more trouble.

But it was, oh, so hard to sit there and wait! To not go running out into the gathering night to find him.

Hannah put the lamp she carried down on the table and only then did Jane notice how dark it had become in the room.

'You have a caller, my lady,' Hannah said.

'A caller?' Jane said, surprised. For just an instant she was sure it was Hayden, but then she felt silly. He wasn't a 'caller', he lived there—or so she had begun to imagine. 'At this time of day?'

'It's Sir David Marton, my lady. Shall I tell him you're not at home?'

Jane shook her head wearily. That disappointment that Hayden hadn't returned lingered, but she hadn't seen Sir David in several days, not since their walk to the village. Perhaps he could be a welcome distraction. 'No, show him in. Is Miss Emma still in her chamber?'

'Yes, my lady. I just left her some tea.' Hannah paused, shuffling her feet. 'And I haven't seen Lord Ramsay come back yet.'

'Thank you, Hannah.' As the maid left, Jane went to the looking glass and tried to tidy her hair, to erase the marks of the long, strange day. She gave up after a moment, seeing it was a lost cause.

'Lady Ramsay,' Sir David greeted her as he entered the room. He gave her a bow. 'I hope you're doing well. Louisa has been complaining she hasn't seen you in ages. She says you must come to tea next week.'

'It has been rather busy here, I'm sorry to say, but hopefully very soon all will return to normal here at Barton,' Jane answered. 'It's good to see you again, Sir David.'

And it was good to see him. He seemed like a spot of calm, a sign of the orderly life she had once fashioned for herself and Emma here at Barton that had been so disturbed lately. She invited him to sit by her on the sofa and tell her of all the local doings she had missed. Soon he had her laughing at a tale of the vicar's cow getting loose from the vicarage yard and running amok around the church and she almost forgot Carstairs and the others. Even the usually solemn Sir David laughed as he told her about it.

They were still laughing when Hayden strode into the room. 'Sir David,' he greeted abruptly, his glance flickering between Jane and their guest as he frowned.

Really, that is too unfair, Jane thought, considering the trouble his friends had caused of late. Her friends were nothing compared to that. She wiped the tears of laughter from her eyes and said, 'Sir David has brought greetings from his sister and an invitation to tea next week.'

'I had no idea tea invitations were so mirthful,' Hayden said.

'Oh, no, we were only laughing at a story about the vicar's cow,' she said. 'That is nothing to London repartee, of course, but rather amusing to us locals. Perhaps you'd care to hear it, Hayden?'

As Sir David obligingly told the story again, Jane went to pull the bell to send for some tea. Suddenly, something outside the window caught her attention, some sudden flare of light in the gathering darkness.

'How strange,' she murmured, and as she hurried to investigate Hayden and Sir David broke off their tense conversation to follow her.

'What is it?' Hayden asked, peering over her shoulder.

'I'm not sure. I thought I saw something.' The garden looked peaceful again, quiet and sleeping. She started to turn away, but a sudden burst of orange-red light shot up above the walls of the maze.

'Fire!' she screamed, spinning towards the door in a rush of fear.

Hayden and Sir David were already running out of the room. Jane dashed after them. Surely the earth was damp enough to contain any flames, but the horrible image of the gardens and house blackened and crumbling loomed in her mind.

As the men rushed into the garden, Jane hurried downstairs and grabbed the basket of linen waiting to be washed. Maybe she could use it to smother some of the flames.

'Fetch help from the village!' she called to Hannah and ran back into the hall.

When she got into the garden, the air was tinged with the sharp, metallic smell of smoke. As she ran down the pathway, the terrible visions faded and she could only hear the roar of her heartbeat in her ears, the rush of frantic activity all around her.

The fire was flaring higher and higher at the centre of the maze. Smoke rolled towards her like a silver-grey wall, stinging her eyes and burning her lungs. She could barely see the figures of Hayden and David Marton ahead of her.

Jane quickly dug out a handkerchief from her apron pocket and tied it over her nose, then she ran into the very centre of the maze. The flames were spreading from the overgrown flowerbeds, licking at the wooden walls of the old summerhouse. If they didn't get it under control, she knew they would spread to the hedge walls and out to the rest of the garden.

She dived towards the outermost edges of the flames and beat at them with one of the sheets. The heat prickled on her skin, tiny pinpricks of searing steel, and her eyes watered until she could hardly see, but still she fought on. She had to. This was her home.

She managed to put out one fire and spun around to beat at another. The figures of the men, ghostly and faint, mere blurry outlines, slid in and out of view through the smoke. She was vaguely aware of shouts, of more people running into the clearing, but all she could do was keep fighting. Keep fighting even though her arms ached as if they would wrench away from her shoulders, even though she couldn't breathe.

She fought until suddenly her knees collapsed beneath her. Coughing and choking, she fell to the ground, too weak to move. She tried to push herself to her feet, to get away from the horrible, searing heat, and she sobbed in frustration.

Suddenly, strong hands caught her by the shoulders and lifted her up. Jane blinked away the smoke tears to see David Marton standing above her.

'You need to get away from here,' he shouted above the chaos.

She shook her head, but he wouldn't let go of her. He drew her away from the charred ruins of the summerhouse, collapsing in on itself, and made her sit down in a quieter, cooler spot near the hedge. Only then did she see that most of the flames were out. Hayden was beating at the last of them, his white shirt grey and his usually immaculate hair dotted with ash. Hannah and some of the villagers who had no doubt been out in the fields nearby and saw the flames were putting out the smaller fires.

The ground was scorched and seared, the summerhouse in ruins, but it finally looked as if the rest of the garden was safe.

Suddenly it was as if every ounce of frantic fight drained out of Jane and left her shaking. She choked back a sob.

'It's all right now, Lady Ramsay,' David said. He knelt down beside her and she was glad he was there. He was so quiet and steady, just as she'd once thought. 'The fires are out.'

'But how did they start?' she said. She hated how shaky she sounded. Despite the heat of the flames, she couldn't stop shivering. 'The ground is still so damp...'

David took off his coat and gently draped it over her shoulders. It smelled of smoke, but she was glad of its comforting warmth.

'I fear it may have been started deliberately,' he said, still so very calm. 'There was broken glass and some old rags near the building. I think it spread from there.'

Jane was shocked. Someone had done this thing deliberately? Here at Barton, which had always been her safe haven? 'Who would do that? That is monstrous! No one could possibly hate us like that...'

Suddenly an image of Ethan Carstairs flashed in her mind. His face twisted in fury as Hayden threw him out of Barton Park. *He* would hate them. And surely he had the evil nature that could do something like this.

'Oh, no,' she whispered. 'How could this have happened? All I wanted here was peace and quiet.' She couldn't hold the tears back any longer. They stung her eyes and she swiped them away.

David silently took a handkerchief from his pocket and carefully dabbed at her cheeks. His simple, kind gesture steadied her and she gave him a wobbly smile.

'You really are very kind, Sir David,' she said. 'You only came here to pay a simple call and instead you have to fight fires and comfort weeping women. How tedious for you.'

He gave her one of his rare smiles and Jane

was astonished to see that it took him from a quietly good-looking man to a dazzlingly handsome one. But still he was not as handsome as Hayden. No man was.

And she feared now she would always think that. She would always compare everyone else unfavourably to her husband. Damn him.

'Perhaps I should change my name to Sir Galahad,' he said with a wry laugh.

Jane laughed with him and when he squeezed her hand comfortingly she let him. It *was* comforting. Not confusing and enflaming and wonderful, like when Hayden touched her.

'I think we have a great deal of work to do here,' she said. 'Finding an arsonist, clearing up this mess.'

'You have plenty of friends to help you, I presume, Lady Ramsay,' he said. 'And when we catch the villain who did this, he will be very sorry indeed.'

Jane swiped away the last of her tears as she studied the scene before her, the smoky, damp pall cast over everything, the huge cleaning-up task before her.

And she found Hayden watching her from across the clearing. He stood there very stiff and still, his eyes narrowed on her. Only then did she realise David Marton's hand was still on her arm. She slid away from him, but it was too late. Hayden had already turned and vanished into the wisps of smoke.

He was touching her.

The man was actually touching Jane. He stared across the blackened clearing at them, sitting so close together, their heads near each other as they whispered together, and at first he couldn't quite believe what he was seeing. Then pure fury roared through him, stoked by the fight in his blood from the fire.

Jane was his wife, damn it all! Maybe their marriage wasn't all it should be, maybe he hadn't beaten it into shape as he half-planned to when he rushed so impetuously to Barton. But still—she was his.

He dropped the bucket in his hand and took an angry stride towards them. He would beat that blasted David Marton, the man who was always so infuriatingly calm and cool, to a bloody stain. Then he would pick Jane up in his arms, carry her into the house and make her see once and for all that she truly belonged to him. That she had to finally give up this nonsense and come back with him to London, come back to their lives there.

But something made him freeze in his tracks and that hot anger froze, too. Marton handed Jane a handkerchief and, as she wiped at her eyes, he spoke quietly in her ear. She gave a little smile and nodded.

Hayden realised with a sword-sharp suddenness that he should *not* go to Jane now. He couldn't give her what Marton could in that moment, what she needed after seeing her garden burning—steady, quiet understanding. All the terrible things that had happened to Jane today were because he had let that London life intrude on what she'd worked so hard to build here at Barton.

She'd run away from what they had together and rightly so. He hadn't seen what she needed, and even if he had he couldn't have given it to her. He could only see his life as it had always been, as his parents' lives had been, and that wasn't enough for Jane.

Maybe she should marry someone like

Marton. But it was too late for that. Too late for them to change.

As he watched Jane smile up at Marton, something inside of him seemed to crack wide open, something he had kept locked away his whole life. He wanted to fall to his knees and howl with the pain of it.

But he just watched as Marton helped Jane to her feet and they left the chaos of the maze together. One long moment ticked past, then another, and the sharp pain faded to a dull, throbbing ache. It could almost be just another part of him now.

Hayden curled his hands into fists. He knew he couldn't fight Marton, couldn't fight the past. Yet as he battled to save Barton Park, one true thing had flashed over him. He didn't just fight to save the house for Jane, he was desperate to save it for himself. Desperate to save all Barton had come to mean to him, because without him even looking, it had become something amazing.

In those few days here with Jane and Emma, Barton had become a home. And that was something worth fighting for as he'd never fought before in his life.

'My lord,' a man called and Hayden turned
to face him.

It was one of the men who had come running from the fields around the village to
fight the fire. All the flames were out now,
but grey, ghostly drifts of smoke still drifted
from the charred grass. The ruined walls of
the old summerhouse swayed in the wind
and the air smelled acrid and foul.

'I'm sorry we couldn't save the building,
my lord,' the man said.

Hayden shook his head. 'It doesn't matter.
The summerhouse can be rebuilt. Everyone
was absolutely splendid. The important thing,
the only thing, was to keep the fire from
spreading.' And losing Barton would have
utterly broken Jane's heart—and Hayden's,
too, if he still had a heart to lose.

'This was found over there, my lord, near
that pile of broken glass.' The man held out
a tiny, flashing gold object. 'Looks valuable.
Someone might be searching for it. One of
your guests, mayhap?'

So everyone knew about his scandalous
guests now? Hayden gave a wry laugh as he
reached for the lost object. Of course they

knew. Life in the environs of Barton were quiet. People like his erstwhile friends would be a rich mine of speculative gossip. One more thing for him to repair.

As he turned the gold object on his palm, he recognised it at once. An old Spanish coin that Ethan Carstairs considered lucky for some unfathomable reason. Hayden had often seen the man take it out and twirl it between his fingers at the card tables.

And it was lost here in the maze. Near where the fire looked to have begun.

'Thank you,' Hayden said tightly. 'I will make very sure it's returned to its owner.'

Chapter Sixteen

It was raining again, the needle-sharp droplets pattering at the window glass as lightning split the night sky and thunder cracked overhead.

Emma felt like she was the only one awake to feel the old house shake with it. Jane took dinner in her room; Emma hadn't seen her since the fire had died down and everyone from the village drifted home. Hayden, too, had vanished, so Emma ate alone in the dining room and then retreated to the library to try to read. She'd neglected her botanical studies too long in the fruitless search for treasure.

But she couldn't quite focus like she once

did. The smell of smoke still hung heavy in
the air, though the fresh rain would surely
banish any lingering sparks. But no storm
could banish the terrible images in her mind,
of looking out the window and seeing the
garden on fire. Of her sister's tear-streaked
face as Sir David Marton helped her into the
house, both of them stained and reeking from
the smoke. Marton had been so solicitous, so
comforting in those moments of chaos.

Emma almost felt bad about thinking him
just a dry old stick.

She buried her face in her hands and listened to the howl of the thunder. Murray laid
his paw on her foot, whining, but she had no
comfort to give him. Barton Park, which had
been her family's refuge for so long, felt like
it was under siege. Ethan Carstairs, the fire,
Jane's sad eyes—Emma just wanted to banish it all, but she couldn't.

Jane had seemed so happy for a few days
and so had Hayden. The angry look in his
eyes when he first came to Barton had faded,
only to come back in force when his friends
showed up. Everything Emma had thought

so sure, so hopeful, had vanished like that smoke outside. She didn't like it at all.

She thought about the treasure she'd been so sure was in the maze. The treasure that would save them, almost as if it was some sort of magical talisman. Maybe the fire would uncover something. But even if the old treasure was found it wouldn't fix anything. Jane and Hayden would still be apart. Emma still would be full of that restless knowledge that she couldn't fix anything.

Emma tossed her pencil down on the open book in front of her and pushed herself back from the desk. Once she'd felt so sure of so many things. Now she knew nothing.

She moved out of the circle of candlelight and into the darkness by the window. Rain poured down in earnest now, battering the abused garden. A quick flash of purplish lightning illuminated the overgrown flowerbeds, the haze of smoke that hung in the dark air.

Suddenly she saw something, a flash of movement in the blackness. It could almost have been a shadow thrown off by one of the old statues, but then it slid away, along the path towards the house. Emma shielded the glare of the window glass with her hands and peered closer, hardly daring to breathe. After everything that had happened today, she feared it could be anything at all.

One more bolt of lightning illuminated a man's face as he ran and she saw it was Ethan Carstairs returned to Barton Park.

'That bloody bastard,' she cried, in a fit of profanity that would have horrified Jane. But she couldn't think of any other way to describe that horrible man. He had attacked her, probably started the fire—and now he was back to cause even more trouble.

Well, Emma wasn't going to allow it.

Without stopping to think, she snatched up a sharp silver letter-opener. She ran out of the library, Murray at her heels, and took a cloak from the hook in the hall. After she tugged its folds around her, she pulled open the front door.

The cold force of the rain drove her back, only for a second, but it was long enough to shake her into seeing what she was doing. Being so impetuous had got her into trouble before. She needed to get help now.

But before she could slam the door and go back, a hand shot out of the darkness and grabbed her by the arm. Hard fingers dug into her skin like sharp steel hooks and yanked her out into the storm.

Terrified, Emma opened her mouth to scream, but another hand clamped hard over her mouth, suffocating her.

'So kind of you to meet me halfway, Miss Bancroft,' she heard Ethan Carstairs say, just before stars exploded behind her eyes and she sank down into blackness.

'No!' Jane sat straight up in bed, disoriented and dizzy. What woke her? Was it the rain and wind lashing at the window? Or something inside her chamber?

Inside her own mind?

Her eyes still itched and stung from the smoke, and she rubbed at them as she took a deep breath. It must have only been a dream, a bad, strange dream brought on by the long day. Her body ached and her mind was still heavy with the sleep that clung around her. She couldn't remember her dream, but surely it involved fire and people she loved hovering on the brink of terrible danger where she couldn't reach them.

Finally her pounding heartbeat slowed and she opened her eyes to see that her bedchamber was just as it was before she fell asleep. Her shawl was tossed over the *chaise* and her half-eaten supper still lay on its tray on the table. The bathtub was still in front of the fireplace, the water grey with soot. The curtains were flung open to reveal the storm beyond her window.

Jane rubbed at her arms through her thin muslin sleeves. She'd fallen asleep in her dress. The wind rushing around the house sounded like screams and it made her shiver.

Just a dream, she told herself sternly. Yet there was something deep inside, some whisper of disquiet, that wouldn't go away.

She had a sudden strong urge to look in on Emma. It had been such a long, horrible day, for Emma more than anyone else. She'd been so quiet after the fire, retreating into her room with Murray.

Jane climbed out of bed and wrapped the shawl tightly around her shoulders before she lit a candle and tiptoed down the corridor. Hayden had retired to the room Lady Marlbury had used and the door was tightly closed. Everything was silent there.

But she couldn't think about Hayden, not now. He had looked so strangely tense and distracted after the fire, they hadn't spoken more than a few words and she almost feared to ask him how he felt. She hurried on to Emma's room. She raised her hand to knock on the door, but it swung open at her touch to reveal an empty space beyond. The bed was turned down, but not slept in.

Jane crept slowly into the room. The air smelled of Emma's light, lemony perfume, but was also cold and deserted. Even Murray wasn't there, his cushion by the window empty. The hair at the back of Jane's neck prickled and her hands went cold.

Don't be silly, she told herself. Emma could be anywhere in the house. She probably just couldn't sleep, after all that had happened, and she was still in the library. But that icy feeling wouldn't go away.

Jane hurried downstairs to the library. A lamp burned on the desk and books and notebooks lay open on its surface, but Emma wasn't there. The rainy night seemed to creep in closer and closer.

She spun around and dashed into the hall, her throat tight with a rush of panic. The door was swinging open, rain leaving the tile floor slick and glossy. Something small and shiny gleamed on the wood of the door.

Filled with the creeping stickiness of dread, Jane moved closer. The rain touched her skin, tiny wet pinpricks, but she didn't even notice that. She saw it was the letter-opener from the library, stabbed into the wood to hold a scrap of paper.

Jane snatched it down and quickly scanned the scrawled words.

The treasure for your foolish sister. Unless you want your garden to burn again. Send Ramsay to the ruined farmhouse outside the village. Carstairs.

'Oh, not again,' Jane whispered. She had thought, hoped, the man was gone for good. Hadn't he done enough to them? Hadn't they been through enough at his hands?

She read quickly over the note again, sure she must have misread it, was imagining things. The treasure? What did he mean?

The old legend of the Barton treasure? That seemed so silly, so ridiculous. Yet if he'd taken Emma, it was so deadly serious.

How could she give him what she didn't have? What didn't even exist, except in her father's imagination?

'Jane? What are you doing down here?'

Jane spun around, startled at the sound of a voice, and slipped in the puddles on the tiles. She leaned against the wall and watched Hayden as he hurried down the stairs. He was in his shirtsleeves, his coat over his arm, his hair rumpled and his face hard with worry.

And suddenly she didn't feel so alone in the world, so adrift in a stormy sea of panic. Hayden had been there to help fight the fire. He was there now.

She held out the note. 'Carstairs took Emma,' she said simply.

She half-expected doubts, questions, statements that the smoke must have addled her brain. She should have known better from Hayden. The Hayden who'd so coldly beaten Carstairs up and thrown him out of Barton for touching Emma. Who'd fought the fire with her to save her home.

The Hayden she suddenly knew she could rely on, no matter what came.

'Blast!' he cursed, that one word a low, swift explosion. He took the note from her hand and read it quickly.

'The ruined farmhouse?' he said, his voice taut, as if he held himself tightly, carefully together, just as she did.

Jane watched as he put on the boots he had left discarded on the floor after the fire and shrugged into his coat. 'It's on the road just before you reach the village, behind the old tollgate. We saw it on our walk that day.'

Hayden nodded and turned to go into the library. Jane followed just as he opened a small trunk of his things that had been left there when he arrived at Barton. He drew an inlaid box from the bottom of the case and Jane recognised it right away. His duelling pistols, kept on a high shelf in the library of the London house. She'd never actually seen him use them, but she had no doubt he could.

He removed one of the pistols and secured it, along with a small bag of shot, inside his coat.

Jane didn't say a word. This Hayden was one she knew could keep her—and Emma—safe.

'Wake up Hannah, so you can start to form a search party,' Hayden said. 'They can ride out after me, while you stay here and keep watch.'

'No!' Jane cried, remembering how frightened Emma was the first time Carstairs attacked her. Once they found her, Emma would need her sister. 'I can't wait here. I'm coming with you.'

Hayden looked up at her with a frown. 'Jane, it's still storming out there. And you've already seen how desperate Carstairs is, what he is capable of.'

'I *am* going. I know the area better than you, Hayden. And Emma is my sister. She—she's going to need me.' Jane held her chin up high, swallowing her tears, swallowing everything but the knowledge that Emma needed her now and she had to be strong. 'If you make me stay behind, I will just follow on my own.'

Hayden gave her a quick flash of a smile. He came to her and took her cold hand tightly in his. He raised it to his lips for a quick kiss, and that warm touch steadied her.

'I know better than to argue with you, Jane,' he said. 'Fine, we will go together. Just stay close to me.'

Jane nodded. Of course she would stay close to him. There was no telling what they would find out there in the storm.

Chapter Seventeen

It was a hellish night.

Hayden couldn't see five feet in front of him in the impenetrable curtain of rain, which drove like relentless tiny needles into his skin. They'd managed to ride Hayden's horse for a while, until the muddy ground forced them to go forwards on foot. Now they walked, the saturated ground sucking at their boots, the wind howling around them, tearing at their clothes.

The lamp Hayden held in one hand did them no good, barely lighting their own faces. His other hand held on to Jane's, her fingers stiff and cold in his. Her pale face, framed by the sodden folds of her hood and beaded with raindrops like tiny diamonds, stared ahead with fierce determination. She was like a furious mother lion whose cub was threatened and, if Hayden didn't hate Carstairs for what the villain had done, he would almost feel sorry for the man. Jane was indomitable when it came to fighting for what she loved.

Once she'd tried to fight for them and he had only driven her away. Given up what could have been theirs. They began with such hope on their wedding day and he just threw it away. Threw away the best thing that had ever happened to him.

But he would find her sister now. He would save the person Jane loved and make sure her life was happy from now on. Even if he couldn't be in it himself.

It was the very least he could do for her.

'Whatever you are trying to do, it won't work,' Emma said. She tried to sound brisk and cool, as Jane did when she was directing something. She couldn't show that she was scared. She *wouldn't*, not to the wild-eyed madman who paced the dirt floor in front of her.

She drew her knees up under her chin and tried not to shiver. The old roof of the ruined farmhouse was mostly gone, but she had managed to find a semi-dry spot under the eaves, where she could huddle out of the rain. Her head hurt where she had hit it on the doorstep when Carstairs grabbed her and she had to fight off waves of dizziness.

She needed all her wits about her now if she was to escape.

'Be quiet, witch,' Carstairs shouted, pacing back and forth, shaking his head madly as if he could cast away this whole ugly night. As if he couldn't quite believe what evil he had done. Emma couldn't believe it, either. Barton was her haven, she could never have imagined such a thing could ever happen there. But it had. She had to stay calm and find a way to get out of there.

How could she ever have thought this man was handsome? How could she have listened to his flattery for even a moment?

She wrapped her arms tighter around herself, as if that could be her armour. On her sash she felt the press of something small and hard, cold through her chemise. It was the pearl circle pin that had once been her mother's, that Jane had given her to comfort her.

Before she could think about it too long, Emma tore it free and leaped to her feet. When Carstairs turned towards her again, she lunged forwards and stabbed him as hard as she could in the temple.

'Bitch!' he roared and reached out for her wildly. His hand struck her on the side of the head and she reeled backwards, but she forced herself to stay upright. She shoved him away and rushed out of the meagre shelter of the old house and into the rain.

Emma ran blindly through the pouring downfall, not knowing for certain where she was going. She heard Carstairs give a roar of fury behind her and it drove her on through the rain.

The mud soaked her thin slippers and she was sobbing with fear, but still she kept running. He was still after her, she knew he was.

She stumbled and fell, landing hard in the cold mud. She held her breath and listened carefully. Her heart thundered in her ears, along with the waters of the river rushing below the slope. Somewhere she could hear Murray barking, faint above the rush of the water. And thunder—and Carstairs shouting her name.

She pushed herself to her feet and ran towards the river.

The old ruined farmhouse was deserted.

Jane stood inside the gaping doorway and stared around the empty space in cold disbelief. She'd been so sure Emma would be there, that this would all end soon. But if her sister had once been here, she was gone. Hayden held up his lamp, his pistol held ready in his other hand, but there was nothing to see.

'Where could she be?' he muttered, his voice thick with an anger and anxiety that matched her own.

She kicked out at the damp dirt floor. A lightning strike caught a sparkle on the floor and Jane knelt to snatch it up. It was Emma's small pearl brooch, the one that had once belonged to their mother.

'They *were* here,' she said.

And then a scream split the night around them.

Emma balanced carefully on the slippery riverbank, the wind tugging at her wet skirts. Her feet were numb, holding her rooted in place. She could still hear the ring of Murray's frantic barks, but she couldn't see him.

She glanced frantically over her shoulder, sure Carstairs must be just behind her. He appeared at the top of the slope, his face white and twisted in the lightning-light.

'You stupid little whore!' he shouted. 'Come back here right now. You've caused me enough trouble and you'll be very sorry for that.'

'No!' she screamed, trying to spin away from him as he reached for her.

'Emma,' she heard Hayden call out of the storm.

She half-turned and glimpsed her brother-in-law through the rain, not far behind Carstairs on the riverbank. She tumbled off balance as Carstairs snatched at her sleeve and she fell backwards in a tumbling blur of confusion and fear. The water caught at her and Carstair's hard hands tried to push her even harder.

Through the haze, she saw Hayden catch Carstairs and ram his fist into the man's jaw, once, twice, driving him back. With a wild shout, Carstairs went tumbling into the rushing river.

Just before Emma plunged into the icy waters after him, Hayden snatched her by the arm and jerked her up and free. He fell to his knees with her, the waves lapping at her skirts, but not close enough to get her.

She wrapped her arms around his neck and clung to him, sobbing. She could feel Hayden trying to rise to his feet, but she was too scared to let go of him. So he knelt there in the mud, holding her.

'It's all right now, Emma,' he said in her ear, the words strong and calm in the midst of the storm. 'He's gone. He can't hurt you now. We're here.'

'H-how do you know?' Emma wailed. She'd been so scared of Carstairs and the crazy, wild light in his eyes. How could he be gone, just like that?

'I saw him swept down the river,' Hayden said. 'I had to pull you out instead.'

Emma nodded against his shoulder. She was still so numb, she could hardly comprehend what had happened. But somewhere in the distance, she heard the echo of a bark and it shook her out of her panic.

'Come on, we must find your sister,' Hayden said. 'She's terrified for you.'

Emma let him help her to her feet. She swayed dizzily, but his arm around her shoulders held her steady.

'Jane is lucky to have you, Hayden,' she said. 'We're both lucky you came here.'

'I doubt Jane would agree with you,' he answered. 'But I'd appreciate it if you could put in a good word for me with her.'

And together they climbed up the steep, slippery riverbank into the light.

Some wild creature was howling like it was wounded, a horrible, mournful sound. Jane clapped her hands over her ears to blot it out, only to realise that the howling was *her*. It was inside her head.

She stood balanced at the top of the riverbank, struggling to see what was happening through the darkness and rain. All she could make out was flashes of sudden, pale movement. Screams and shouts, a dog barking frantically somewhere in the distance. But she couldn't see what was happening to whom, if her husband and sister were still there somewhere.

Suddenly she saw a tall figure go reeling back into the rushing river. He instantly vanished into the water.

'Hayden!' Jane screamed. She took one lurching step forwards, only to trip and fall to her knees. Pain shot up her legs when she landed hard in the rutted mud, but she barely felt it through her fear.

There was a rush of sound, and a small, wet, warm object hit her in the chest. Murray, caked in mud, his ribs heaving, as panicked as she was. She clutched him against her, trying frantically to see what was happening down at the river. For a second she closed her eyes tightly and whispered a desperate prayer.

Let them be safe...

When she opened them, it was to a wondrous sight. Hayden and Emma were stumbling up the steep bank. Her sister's head rested on her husband's shoulder, her golden hair trailing around them in tendrils like serpents.

Jane had never seen anything more beautiful than the two of them, soaked through and covered with mud, but alive. The people she loved. Her family.

She scrambled to her feet and raced to throw her arms around them, Murray at her heels. 'You're alive, you're alive,' she sobbed, over and over.

'I'm sorry, Jane,' Emma cried. 'I never…'

'Hush,' Jane whispered. She kissed Emma's cheek, then Hayden's, just letting herself look at them, letting herself know they were all there. 'You're alive. We're together. That's all that matters now.'

And in that moment, fear still humming in her veins, cold rain pouring down on their heads, she knew that was true. It was the *only* truth. They were together. That was all that ever mattered.

'Jane…'

'Hush, don't say anything, Hayden,' Jane

said as she hurried to open the bedroom door
and help her husband to the bed. She tried
to be brisk, nurse-like, to not show him her
fear that he was bleeding. He was hurt, hurt
trying to save her sister, and she had to be
strong for him. Even though inside she was
terrified.

Terrified she would lose him now, when
she had only just found him again.

She urged him to lie back on the pillows.
'Sir David has gone to fetch the doctor, he
will be here very soon. You must rest until
then.'

'Emma?' he asked hoarsely.

'She is safe now. The doctor will see to
her, too.'

Hannah hurried in with a tray in her
hands, a basin of steaming water and pile of
clean cloths. Jane wrung one out and carefully dabbed at the worst of the bleeding cuts
on Hayden's face.

He suddenly reached up and grabbed her
hand, holding her tightly. 'Don't leave me,'
he said.

'Oh, Hayden,' she said, her throat tight.
She felt tears prickle at her eyes and she

couldn't do anything but let them fall. 'Don't you know by now? I could never leave you again. I was so silly and foolish when we first met, I didn't know what marriage was.'

'I was the foolish one. I couldn't see then what you really offered.'

What had she offered him, compared to what he could give her? She had loved him, or thought she did anyway, but it had never amounted to all she had hoped for. 'What did I give you? I had nothing then, just my own fanciful dreams.'

He pressed a quick, fervent kiss to her hand. 'You had everything. Love, a family, a home. All things I never had and never realised I *could* have. I saw your gentle spirit when we first met and I wanted it for myself. But just as you said, I didn't know what that meant. I was selfish.'

Jane's tears were falling now in earnest, splashing over their joined hands. She had once dreamed he would say this to her, would mean it, and now it was really happening. She thought her heart would burst. 'What went wrong for us, Hayden?'

'We just weren't ready for each other, my

love. But I swear I will be a true husband to you now. I will spend every day making sure you are happy. If you will only let me.'

She wanted that so very much it hurt. It seemed she had been waiting so, so long to know he meant his words and for her to be ready to fully return them. She loved Hayden. She had loved him since the moment they met, but since he came to Barton that love had deepened, ripened.

Yet still a hard, cold kernel of fear lingered.

'What about the babies?' she choked out, and that was all she could say. The pain and fear of their lost children lingered like ice in those words.

And Hayden seemed to hear it all and understand it. He bowed his head over her hand. 'We can try again, make it work. Or if you can't, if the doctor says you should not, we'll let my blasted cousin have the title. I don't care, Jane. I only want you. *Only* you. Please…'

Suddenly he groaned. His hands fell from hers and he collapsed to the bed, unconscious.

Fear pierced through Jane, sharper than any sword. 'Hayden!' she cried. 'No, no. Come back to me, please. I love you, too. Please, please...'

But all she heard were her own pleading words, echoing back to her. Hayden was silent.

Chapter Eighteen

Jane paced the length of the corridor, and sat down in the chair at the end, and then jumped up to pace all over again. She couldn't be still, couldn't stop and think. Whenever she stopped moving, the whole nightmare reeled through her mind again. The lightning, the rushing rain, the screams. Hayden stumbling up the slippery riverbank with Emma in his arms.

The men from the village said Carstairs's body had been pulled from the river, with roughly sketched, sodden maps of the Barton garden in his pocket. It was something of a relief to know the man would never trouble them again, but still her mind would not be calm.

Jane looked for the hundredth time towards Hayden's closed chamber door. How long had the doctor been in there? It seemed like hours. Hayden hadn't wanted to let the doctor tend him when the man came to look in on Emma, but Jane had insisted. Hayden was limping on the leg he injured when he first came to Barton and there was a deep cut on his forehead. Now they'd been in there for too long.

What if there was some terrible injury, some bleeding inside where it couldn't be seen? What if—what if she lost him again? This time for good?

Just the thought of it all, of Hayden being somewhere she could never say she was sorry, she was wrong, was utterly unbearable.

She sat down hard on the chair and closed her eyes against the pain in her head. She tried to force the fear away and imagine good things again. Hayden laughing with Emma in the garden. Hayden across the dinner table from her, smiling at her in the candlelight. Hayden in her bed, touching her, kissing her.

The peace they had found here for such brief days. The peace, the family, she had wanted all along, and lost in misunderstandings and anger. Surely it couldn't be gone for ever?

'Jane?' she heard Emma say softly. She opened her eyes to find her sister standing at the end of the corridor, Murray cradled in her arms. She still looked pale and startled, bruises standing out in stark purple relief against her white skin.

Jane pushed herself to her feet. 'Are you all right, Emma? You're supposed to be resting.'

'I can't possibly sleep.' Emma glanced at Hayden's door. 'Is the doctor still there?'

'Yes. I haven't heard anything yet.'

Emma nodded. 'I— Will Hayden leave again, do you think?'

'I don't know,' Jane answered truthfully. She didn't know what was in Hayden's mind after all that had happened. He seemed happy here at Barton. But maybe now he missed his old London life, the one his friends brought to their doorstep. The one a woman like Lady Marlbury could give him.

'I don't want him to go,' Emma said, her

voice thick, as if she held back tears. Murray whined up at her. 'He isn't at all what I once thought he was.'

'No, he isn't.' Jane's husband was at once more complex and far simpler than she ever could have imagined.

'I thought I could help us by finding the Barton treasure,' Emma said. 'But I see now I didn't need it. Our treasure is right here, isn't it? It's us.'

'Yes,' Jane murmured, smoothing her hand over her sister's hair. 'Yes, our treasure is in us.'

The bedchamber door suddenly opened, and the doctor emerged with his valise in hand. Jane leaped up and Emma grabbed her hand.

'How is he?' Jane asked tightly.

The doctor shook his head. 'Lord Ramsay certainly gets battered around a bit, doesn't he, my lady? He has some cuts and bruises, and I certainly recommend rest for several days at least, but there should be no permanent damage.'

Jane let out the breath she was holding as relief rushed through her. *No permanent damage*. Hayden was still alive; he *would* live. There was still hope. 'Thank you, Doctor.'

The doctor gave them a stern glance before he turned towards the stairs. 'I think a seaside holiday would be in order for all of you, Lady Ramsay. A month or two at Brighton would do you some good. Or even better—Italy.'

'Italy.' Emma sighed. 'Wouldn't it be wonderful if Hayden took us to Italy, Jane? I could find so many new plant specimens there.'

Jane had to laugh. Yes, it *would* be splendid. A long, sunny holiday, just the three of them, away from all that had happened. A fresh start.

If only Hayden wanted it, too.

'I should go look in on him,' Jane said, reaching for the door handle. 'You should rest, Emma.'

'Yes, of course,' Emma said, already distracted now. 'Just as soon as I find some books on Italy in the library...'

As Emma dashed down the stairs, Jane stepped into the darkened bedchamber. The curtains were drawn across the windows, blocking out the greyish daylight, and two lamps burned on the dressing table. A tray with a pitcher of water and discarded bandages was on the bedside table, and the sicksweet smell of medicine and woodsmoke hung in the air.

Hayden lay in the centre of the bed, blankets and pillows piled around him in copious heaps. Hannah had been very solicitous towards him since he got home. His black hair was stark against the white linens, his eyes closed.

They opened when Jane clicked the door shut behind her and he watched her from across the room as she tiptoed closer.

'How do you feel?' she asked.

A faint smile touched his lips. 'As if I did ten rounds at the boxing saloon—and lost.'

That smile made Jane want to cry. She'd been so afraid she might never see it again, might never have the chance to be with him and tell him…

'I'm so sorry, Hayden,' she whispered.

His smile drifted into a frown. 'What do you mean? Jane, this was all my fault.

I let Carstairs into the house, even though I never liked him. *You* have nothing to be sorry about.'

Jane hurried across the room and carefully sat down on the edge of the bed. She could feel Hayden watching her intently, but she stared down at her clasped hands in her lap and tried to decide how to tell him what she had to say. The confusion that had plagued her for days had suddenly cleared and she could see everything she should have known all along.

Everything she wanted—if it was still there for her. If it wasn't lost for ever.

'I loved you so much when we married, Hayden,' she said quietly. 'I'd never known anyone, anything, like you. So full of life, like a whirlwind. I was dazzled by you, by what I thought you were.'

'Are you saying you were deceived then, that you thought you loved me but you no longer do?'

Jane heard the confusion and pain in his voice, even though he tried to conceal them. She remembered what he told her about his family, about how he could never be good enough for them to love him, and her heart ached.

'No!' she protested. She turned to him and stared into his eyes, those beautiful blue eyes that seemed to contain the whole world. 'I am saying—back then I was young and foolish. I thought marriage would be perfect, easy, and when it wasn't I didn't know what to do. I was frightened. I loved a dream that could never be true. But now I love the reality, Hayden. I love *you*.'

And when she said those words she saw how very simple it all was after all. She loved Hayden. She loved what he'd fought against inside himself and won, loved how he had come for her, loved the life she saw now they could have here at Barton. When he had risked his life for her and for Emma, she'd known her first instincts when she met him and fell for him had been right after all.

She loved him, She didn't want to lose him again.

But what if he didn't feel the same?

'I love you,' she said again, throwing herself off the cliff. 'I want us to be married again, to make a true life together. Here at

Barton, in London—it doesn't matter. I just want to be your wife again.'

For a long, tense moment, he was silent. He stared at her, his eyes unreadable. Just as Jane started to turn away, sure that it was too late, his arms came close around her and he drew her against him.

'Damn it all, Jane, if I'm asleep and dreaming don't let anyone wake me up,' he said. 'I never thought I would hear you say those words again. I thought you were gone for ever. The mistakes I made, the stupid mistakes...'

Jane laughed and cried all at once, holding on tightly to Hayden as he kissed her over and over. 'We have both made mistakes, both been in pain. But we can make a new start now, if that is what you want, too.'

Hayden drew back, holding her face tenderly between his hands as he stared down at her. 'It's all I want. I love you, Jane. I want to show you how much, show you that I've changed. I can be the husband you deserve now. Let me prove that.'

'You don't have to prove anything to me.

We just have to be together now,' Jane said. 'Together always.'

'Always,' he said, and there was the ring of deepest, truest promise in that one word. As if he was making his vows to her all over again. As if their marriage now was truly begun.

Always. This time, Jane knew that word was the whole world. She was Hayden's now, and he was hers. Always.

Epilogue

Lake Como—one year later

'Jane, look!'

Jane glanced up from the book she had balanced on the marble balustrade of the terrace and shielded her eyes from the sunlight to wave at Emma. Her sister dashed along the lakeshore, the hem of her white muslin dress wet as she threw sticks into the water for Murray. The dog, who'd grown prodigiously large on the good Italian food, joyfully dived into the waves as Emma clapped.

Jane waved and laughed, feeling more contented than she ever would have thought possible as she saw Emma having so much fun. After her kidnapping, Emma had grown so quiet and withdrawn, wandering around the gardens alone, waking at night from bad dreams, until Jane feared for her health. That was when Hayden suggested they follow the doctor's advice and take an Italian holiday.

There, under the azure skies and brilliant sun, the flowers and the good food, Emma began to blossom again. She laughed and chatted, just as she had before all the bad things happened. And, if possible, she'd even grown more beautiful. The young English bucks on their Continental tours followed her about every time she went to tour a museum or a ruin, sending flowers and letters, asking Hayden for her hand in marriage.

But Emma just dismissed them with a laugh and went on about her studies. There would be time to worry about her marriage later. Right now Jane was just glad she was happy and healthy.

And Emma wasn't the only one growing and blooming under the Italian sun. Jane rested her hand gently on her own belly, now large and rounded, and felt the baby stir under her touch. It liked to move about, kicking and turning restlessly as if her little son or daughter couldn't wait to be out in the world.

Jane smiled as she felt a tiny foot press into her palm. At first, she had lain awake worrying this child would be lost before it even had a chance to see the sun, just as her other babies had. When she'd lost that last baby, so much hope had slipped away with it, and she and Hayden were pushed even further apart.

But this child had grown and thrived, and in a few weeks she would hold it in her arms. Even if something terrible happened, she knew now she needn't fear—Hayden was with her. They were truly together now and nothing could push them apart. This last year had shown her that every day. Their love for each other grew every day, content and peaceful. They had married too young, expected too much of each other, but now they were ready for their life together. Truly ready.

'What is Emma up to now?' she heard Hayden say. She glanced back to see him coming out the open terrace doors, a platter of fruit in his hand. He had turned golden in the sun, his dark hair slightly lighter, and his smile gleamed.

It made Jane smile, too. 'She's running in the water like a hoyden, of course.'

Hayden laughed and sat down on the *chaise* next to her. He popped a glistening strawberry between her lips. Its sweetness burst on her tongue, as perfect as the day.

'I had another suitor beg me for permission to marry her this morning,' he said. 'It seems there's a line out the door every day.'

'I know.' Jane sighed. 'Yet she cares for none of them.'

'There is time for her to find the right one. None of these gadabouts are good enough.'

'I hope so. I want her to be as happy as we are one day.'

'No one could possibly be as happy as we are.' Hayden smiled and leaned over to kiss her, his lips sweeter than the strawberries, the sunlight. Sweeter than anything in the world.

It had been a long, rocky road to get here, full of storms and wrong turns. But it had led them here, to this perfect moment. To a future together, as a family.

Jane gently touched Hayden's cheek and smiled up at him. 'You're absolutely right. No one is as happy as we are.'

* * * * *

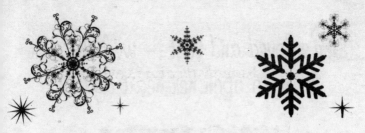
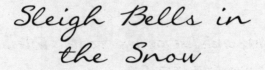

She's loved and lost — will she ever learn to open her heart again?

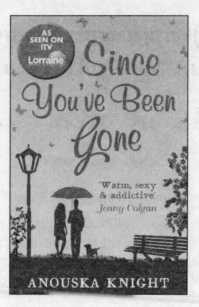

From the winner of ITV Lorraine's Racy Reads, Anouska Knight, comes a heart-warming tale of love, loss and confectionery.

'The perfect summer read — warm, sexy and addictive!'
—Jenny Colgan